The Ex Games
(The Full Series)

J. S. Cooper & Helen Cooper

D1444458

CONTENTS

BOOK 1
CHAPTER 1

"It's one weekend, Katie. You'll survive." Meg giggled at the expression on my face. "I mean, it can't be that bad...can it?"

"It's going to be worse than bad," I groaned and flopped down on her bed. "I may die. I mean it. I may literally die of embarrassment."

"You won't die. You may be embarrassed though." She gave me a sympathetic smile.

"I can't believe this is happening to me." I buried my head in her pillow. "Of all the jobs in all of the world, I had to get this one."

"You were happy about it a few weeks ago."

"That was before I heard about this weekend training." I groaned and stared up at her. "I had no idea he worked for Marathon Corp."

"Well, he more than works for them now." She laughed, and I shuddered.

"I should quit. I'm going to quit!" I cried out melodramatically. "You'll have to take care of the rent for the next few months while I look for a job. I'll cook and clean and be your house woman."

"Yeah, right. You can't cook or clean for shit." Meg

collapsed next to me onto the bed and rubbed my shoulder. "And you know I'm saving up for my trip."

"You're not really going to travel around the world and leave me, are you?"

"You can always come with me."

"But I have a job," I whined and saw her grinning at me. "Fine, I'm not quitting. This is the job I've been waiting for my whole life. I'm not quitting just because he owns the company."

"Hear ye, hear ye."

"Don't go being a lawyer on me," I moaned at her, and she laughed.

"I didn't go through three years of law school to just stop." She jumped up off the bed and grabbed my hands. "Come on, lazy bones. Let's go shopping. You may as well look hot when you see him."

"I don't want to see him. Maybe he'll have forgotten me." The thought sent a ripple of hurt through me.

"There's no way he will have forgotten you."

"He's going to hate me." I gave her a pained expression. "Or he's going to fire me."

"He dumped you. He's not going to hate you." Meg brushed her long blonde hair as she waited for me to get up. "And we're going to make him regret it."

"Why oh why did Brandon Hastings have to buy Marathon Corp?" I slowly dragged myself off of the bed and looked into the vanity mirror. I wasn't altogether displeased with my appearance, but I wished I didn't look quite so washed out. My long brown hair looked messy, but that was nothing a brush couldn't fix. I examined my face and was pleased that my brown eyes looked bright and cheerful even though I was filled with inner turmoil.

"You look gorgeous, Katie."

"I look like a little kid," I groaned. "I don't look like a manager."

"Hey, it's not your fault you're super smart. So what if you're twenty-five and an executive manager already?

2

Anyone who cares about that is just jealous."

"Brandon will care." I sighed and I bit my lower lip as I grew serious and put my face in my hands. "Oh my God, Meg, what am I going to do?"

"It's all in the past, Katie. You made a mistake. He can't be holding a grudge for all these years."

"It was a pretty big mistake." I made a face. "Some may even say it was a lie."

"Well, it was a lie." Meg made an apologetic face as she spoke honestly. "But it was seven years ago."

"Yeah." I straightened my shirt and pushed my shoulders back like my mother had taught me. "I'm sure he's not thinking about some silly girl he dated seven years ago."

"You were eighteen, new to love! These things happen."

"Yeah." I nodded in agreement. "If he had half a brain, he would have figured it out."

"Exactly." Meg linked her arm through mine and we walked to the living room. "He's the one that broke your heart."

"Exactly." My heart beat slowly as I remembered the tears I had cried late at night. I had been devastated when Brandon dumped me right before Christmas in the first semester of my first college year. Absolutely devastated. I hadn't been able to sleep or eat for weeks. He had made my second semester of college absolutely awful. It wasn't until the summer and a trip to London with my parents that I was finally able to accept that what we'd had was forever gone. He had been my first lover and my first love, but to him, I was just a little girl playing around in fairytale land.

***

Flying in first class was a perk of my job that I loved, even though this was the only time I had actually traveled first class. I sat back in the wide leather seat and looked out the window, trying to lose my thoughts in the clouds. I felt worried as I tried to relax and thought about what was going to happen this weekend. I had only been working for Marathon Corp for about a month. It was the first job that made me feel like a real professional, and I felt like I was going to be fired already.

I was in charge of the whole New England area, and I knew that most, if not all, of the lower managers below me felt that I wasn't qualified for the job. I myself had been amazed when I had been hired as an executive manager. I knew I had the degrees for the job—marketing BA from Columbia and a business management master's degree from NYU. But I didn't have that much experience—only the summer internships I'd done while getting my master's. But I had brains and verve and a lot of initiative. And I knew that I was good at my job. However, I knew that there was no way in hell Brandon would allow me to stay if he realized who I was.

I mean, there was a chance he wouldn't recognize me. It had been seven years, and we had only dated for five months. It had been the best five months of my life, but for him, I bet it was nothing. I also knew that I looked more mature now and definitely dressed like a woman who knew the world. My usually wavy brown hair was flat-ironed straight and I had on mascara and eye shadow. I looked nothing like the girl I'd been when I started college.

Then I had been bright eyed, with minimal makeup and no hair products taming my normally wild hair. Thinking back, it should have been obvious to Brandon that I had been lying, but I knew it was hardly his fault that I had deceived him. I hadn't meant to. It had just been one white lie. I hadn't expected him to ask me out. I hadn't expected to fall in love with him.

I sighed as I remembered the first time I saw Brandon Hastings outside the bar. That night was one of the best in my life. Meg and some other girls had convinced me to join them at a bar in the Lower East Side that they knew didn't card minors if they wore short enough skirts and red enough lipstick. I remembered the day clearly. It was a beautiful, warm August day, not too hot, and we were all excited to be starting college. None of us had lived in New York before, and we were all pretty naïve and green. I don't think that any of us had really had boyfriends in high school because we'd all been too busy studying, trying to earn our way into an Ivy League school. And it had paid off for all of us—we were incoming freshmen at Columbia University, and I think the giddiness that had taken over our lives came to fruition that night.

It was a Friday, the weekend before orientation classes were going to start, so one of the girls had the bright idea of christening our first week before classes started. I had never had any alcohol before and was as eager as the rest to go out and party. We were in New York, so why shouldn't we party it up? We'd all dressed up in the shortest skirts and the tightest tops we owned. I'd borrowed high heels from Meg and a bunch of makeup, and we took the 1 train to 42nd Street and then caught a cab to Doug's.

Doug's was everything I had imagined it was going to be: dark and musty, with bright lights and lots of cool-looking people. I was amazed that we had been able to walk right in without even a second glance from the bouncer. Our plan had worked. None of us were carded, and we walked quickly to the bar to get some drinks. Felicity, who was the one who told us about the bar, ordered us our first round of drinks. Scotch on the rocks. It tasted awful, and I thought my stomach was on fire as it burned slightly.

"That's just to get us buzzed faster," she grinned before ordering a round of Sex on the Beaches. "These will taste better, girls."

And she had been right. I guzzled two glasses down within half an hour, not thinking anything of it, as they hadn't tasted alcoholic at all. We were all just standing around when the DJ started playing some old Madonna songs and Meg grabbed my hand and we ran to the dance floor, giggling. The other girls followed quickly and we danced around as if we were on *Dancing With The Stars*.

We danced all night, and even though different guys came up to us, we turned them down. That wasn't a night for us to look for guys, but a night for us to bond with each other. It was the first of many memories we were going to make together.

We stumbled out of the bar at about one a.m. I remember that Meg and Felicity went to look for a cab while the other girls went to the bathroom. I stood there waiting outside the club and leaning against the wall, feeling dizzy and sick. The evening air was cool, and I shivered in my lack of clothing.

"Are you okay?" The voice was deep and husky, and I remember feeling comforted even though I hadn't been able to look up. "Do you need me to take you somewhere?" The voice was closer this time, and I felt warm hands on my shoulders as he forced me to look up at him.

"I'm fine." I giggled and looked up at him through my fake eyelashes. "Just waiting on my friends."

"You're drunk." He frowned and looked around. "It looks like your friends have left you."

"No, they're in the ladies' room." I pointed toward Doug's. "I'm just waiting on them to come out.

"I see." He stared down at me and there was concern in his blue eyes. "I'll wait with you."

"Thank you." I smiled at him and then started laughing.

"What's so funny?" He frowned as he looked at me and I pointed at his face. "My face is funny?" He gave me a wry smile and I shook my head.

"You look like Clark Gable."

6

"You think so?"

"Yes." I grinned at him. "You're handsome."

"Why, thank you." He looked at his watch then back at me. "We will give your friends a few minutes then see about getting you home."

"Are you trying to seduce me?" I wiggled my eyebrows at him and giggled. He was handsome and I was enjoying flirting with him. His blue eyes were bright and had a wise look. His hair was jet black and contrasted well with his olive skin. He was tall and muscular and smelled like some expensive cologne I didn't know the name of. It certainly wasn't the same cologne my dad or any of my high school boy friends used.

"No, dear." He shook his head. "I don't take advantage of young women."

"You wouldn't be taking advantage of me." I licked my lips slowly. I'd read an article in Cosmopolitan that said the way to seduce a guy was to show him your tongue. "I'm twenty-two. I make my own decisions," I lied easily.

"Well, maybe we can go out when you're sober, and if you still want me to seduce you then, I'll see what I can do." He put his arm around me and his fingers felt like heaven against my skin. "You're cold. Why don't you have a coat?"

"I didn't realize how cold it would get."

"You girls these days don't know how to take care of yourselves." He looked at me disapprovingly, and I wondered how old he was. He definitely wasn't a college student like me. There was no boyish look to him. He was all man, and 100% hunk at that.

"I don't feel good." All of a sudden my head felt like it was going to explode and my stomach was swirling like a hurricane.

"My apartment is just a couple of blocks down if you want to come."

"I don't know," I mumbled as I grabbed his arm. I didn't want to think about anything. I just wanted to lie down on something cool and rest my head so the world would stop spinning.

"Come. I won't hurt you." He took my hand, and I followed him to his apartment. I know, I know—I was a dumbass. If I hadn't been drunk, I would have told him where to get off, but I wasn't in my right mind. I always thought that if only I hadn't been drunk that night, everything might have been different.

I don't really remember much of what happened later that night. It's all a blur in my mind. The next thing I remember after leaving with him is waking up in a king-sized bed, feeling like someone was banging nails into my head.

"Good morning, sunshine," a deep, warm voice greeted me, and I looked up to see him staring down at me with a cup of tea in his hand. "Drink this. I'm cooking breakfast for you right now. Lots of bacon and eggs."

"Ugh, don't talk about food," I groaned and lay back down, my brain racing a million miles a minute. Who was the gorgeous man next to me, and what was I doing in his bed?

"I'm Brandon, by the way." He smiled at me gently. "We didn't exchange names last night."

"Oh." I peeked up at him and swallowed hard. He was gorgeous, and even though I felt like death warmed up, I was still attracted to him.

"And your name is?"

"Oh, sorry. I'm Katie."

"Nice name." He smiled at me again. "Rest a little and I'll be back."

"Okay, thanks." I gave him a quick smile, lay back, and closed my eyes. *Oh my God, oh my God, have I been kidnapped?* I peeked under the sheets and groaned as I saw myself wearing only my bra and panties. He'd taken off my clothes. Then panic hit me—had we had sex? *Oh, God, did I have sex for the first time and not even know it?*

"Scrambled eggs, bacon, and lots of buttered white

toast." He walked back into the room. "Nothing healthy, but it will help your hangover."

"I feel like shit," I blurted out and blushed when I realized what I'd said.

"Not surprising." He laughed. "First hangover?"

"Yeah." I nodded and felt my face going red. Did he know it was the first time I'd ever had a drink as well?

"I don't know many people who've reached the age of twenty-two and never had a drink."

"Oh?" I looked down at the plate and swallowed hard. *Should I tell him the truth?*

"Were you and your friends celebrating something?"

"Yes. Yes we were."

"Oh?" He looked at me expectantly, waiting for an answer. I knew there was no way in hell that I could tell him that we were celebrating starting college. Then the questions would start, the 'Why were you drinking?' and 'Why are you so irresponsible?' I stared at him guiltily. I felt bad and disappointed in myself. I knew that my parents back home in Florida would be upset if they knew I was already making bad choices.

"Sorry, I feel a little sick." I turned my face away from him as I felt myself becoming hypnotized by his blue eyes.

"Do you need to go to the bathroom?"

"Huh?"

"To throw up?"

"Oh, no, no." I shook my head and groaned. "I just need to lie down again."

"Sure. Feel free." He sat next to me on the bed. "Do you mind if I lie down next to you?"

"No," I whispered. My heart was beating fast again and little men were jumping around in my stomach.

"Are you new to the city?"

"Yeah, I moved here from Florida a few weeks ago, for, uh, a job." Technically I wasn't lying. I was going to college to get a job.

"Oh nice. Where are you working?"

"Ooh, my head," I groaned and rolled over, trying to control my panicked breathing. I hated lying and was already regretting my comments. I felt his hand rubbing my back and I froze. What was he doing?

"You're very trusting to be here with me, Katie. I'm not sure where in Florida you're from, but there are a lot of wolves in New York, and they are looking to prey on young girls in their twenties like you."

"I can take care of myself," I mumbled and turned over.

"You're lucky I'm a nice guy." He chuckled, and I looked up at him, not sure if he was joking or being serious. He looked even more handsome close up. His blue eyes were shrewd, and I felt like he could see right through me.

"Yes, thank you."

"I could kiss you right now." His voice sounded like a growl, and my eyes widened. "Don't worry, sweet thing. I'll let you get better first."

"First?" I swallowed.

"That's if you don't have anything against men in their thirties?"

"No, no, of course not," I squeaked out. Thirty wasn't that old. I mean, he wasn't old enough to be my dad.

"Good. I don't normally go for girls in their twenties, but you seem different." His eyes crinkled and he laughed. "That is, if you let me take you on a date."

"You want to take me on a date?" I stammered in shock. Was I dreaming? This seriously good-looking man wanted to take me out?

"I think you're someone I want to get to know better, Katie." He nodded as he looked at me seriously.

"Thank you," I mumbled with a wide smile. I didn't bother to hide my excitement from him. I didn't know then that you aren't supposed to let a guy know that you have feelings for him.

"You're welcome, my dear. You're very welcome." He

jumped off of the bed then and grabbed the plate. "Try and get some more sleep, and we'll see how you feel when you wake up."

"Okay." I nodded sleepily and closed my eyes again. Sleep found me easily and I stretched in the luxurious bed, imagining Brandon's lips kissing me softly.

***

"Ma'am, would you like anything else to drink?" The flight attendant tapped me on the arm and I broke out of my reverie.

"No, thanks." I smiled at her and rubbed my forehead. I was starting to get a headache and a small heartache as well. I hated remembering the first days after I met Brandon because he had been so sweet and wonderful. He had been a man I'd thought only existed in romance novels. The beginning of our relationship was magical. It was only the end that was the stuff that nightmares are made of.

"Okay, just let me know if you change your mind."

"Thanks." I smiled. "Do you know how many more hours until we land in San Francisco?"

"It'll be about two more hours, Ms. Raymond."

"Thanks." I looked back out the window and thought about Brandon again. Maybe I wouldn't even see him. I'm sure he will be busy with the board of directors. What time will he have for a manager? It was just my luck that he had bought the company I worked for. Out of all the companies in the world, he'd had to pick mine. What sort of bad luck was that? He was going to fire me, I just knew it. He would take one look at me, laugh in my face, and fire me. Maybe after calling me a liar. And what could I say? What would I tell HR? I knew the answer to that. I would just leave with my tail between my legs. Because it would be true. I had lied to him.

At first, I'd had a reason, but then I had built up the lie, making everything more complicated. And then it had all exploded in my face. I closed my eyes again and thought of Brandon—my sexy, hunky Brandon.

***

"How was your day today?" His voice was warm and I smiled into the phone.

"Good, what about yours?"

"Long." He groaned. "I don't want to talk about it. I'd rather talk about our dinner tomorrow night. Are you excited?"

"Yes!" I exclaimed in excitement.

"I love that you don't hide your true emotions. I've dated way too many women in New York who act like they can't stand me."

"That's silly," I said honestly.

Thinking back, he should have realized the truth from our phone calls. Brandon had taken my number before putting me in a cab home the afternoon after he had taken me home. He had wanted me to spend the weekend with him, but I'd known that I had to get back to the dorms or my friends would be mad. He had called me every night since then, and I'd delighted in his phone calls.

He'd made me laugh and feel special. He seemed to really want to know how I was spending my days, and he told me little things about himself as well. He was the only son of a billionaire banker and worked at his father's hedge fund. He hated his job but knew that it was his duty. He owned his apartment in Chelsea, and he had a house in the Hamptons and an apartment in San Francisco. He preferred the West Coast but had to stay on the East Coast due to work. He loved dogs but traveled so much that he thought it was unfair to have one. He loved Mexican food and jazz and collecting first-edition books. He was also thirty-five. When he first told me that, I'd felt my heart stop beating. Thirty-five sounded so much older than me. Thirty-five was old enough to be my dad, if he'd had sex at a young age. Thirty-five made me feel guilty for having him think I was twenty-two, about to turn twenty-three. Thirty-five made me keep my real age a secret. I didn't want to stop talking to him. I didn't want his calls to end, and I very much wanted to go on that dinner date with him. Thirty-five made me realize that I couldn't let him know that I was eighteen, even though I very much wanted to be honest about my age.

"I can't wait to see you tomorrow," he whispered into the phone. "I'm going to take you to dinner and then we can go dancing if you want."

"That would be nice. Do you know what club you're thinking of?" I grabbed my laptop so I could check Yelp to see if they let in people under twenty-one.

"Oh, not a club." He smiled. "I was thinking we could go to some salsa classes."

"Salsa?"

"Yes, you know, the Spanish dance."

"Oh, yeah. I've just never heard of a date where people went to classes."

"What are you used to, Katie? Burgers and movies?"

"Something like that." I laughed.

"Then that just means you've been dating boys, not men like me."

"Yeah, that could be right." If he'd only known just how true his words were.

"Men in their twenties are still chasing the almighty dollar and trying to get laid. Men in their thirties know that money and sex are not important."

"It's not?" I'd had neither and still hoped for both.

"I mean, we need it to live, of course. But it's not worth losing your life for either."

"I suppose that's true."

"So tomorrow, shall I pick you up from your apartment?"

"My apartment?" My body burned as I stared at my roommate's empty bed. "Uh, no. I've got a late day at work tomorrow. I can meet you at the restaurant." I couldn't believe how easily the lies slid from my mouth.

"Okay, that makes sense." He yawned. "Tomorrow will be our first date."

"I know."

"I can't wait to see you again." He chuckled. "And if anyone I knew heard me say that, they'd think someone had stolen my body."

"Why?"

"This isn't me, Katie. I'm not a romantic guy. I don't do relationships."

"Oh, I didn't know." I felt disappointed and confused. "Why are you talking to me then?"

"I don't know. I guess there was something about you that touched me as I walked by."

"You mean my puke?" I joked and he laughed.

"Thank God, no." He cleared his throat. "I'm not really sure why I stopped and took you home though. I've asked myself several times what I was thinking. You could have been a psycho."

"*I* could have been a psycho? *You* could have been a psycho."

"I'm glad neither of us is a psycho."

"Me too. Sweet dreams, Brandon."

"Sweet dreams, Katie."

"Have a good day at work."

"You too."

"Thanks." *I'll be doing the assignment I didn't do tonight because I was waiting for your call.*

"I'll see you tomorrow."

"See you then." And then we hung up. I lay in my bed and hugged my pillow tightly. I was so excited. This was going to be my first proper date and it was with a man who knew the world, and he was interested in *me*. I couldn't believe it. I was worried about what we would talk about. What if I sounded like an idiot?

"You up?" The door creaked and Meg walked in with a handful of books.

14

"Yeah." I sat up and looked at her with a guilty pang. I hadn't studied all week. It was only the first week, but I knew I had to keep up or I was going to fail out. Everyone in my class at Columbia was smart, and they all seemed to know more than I did. There was no way I was going to be able to sail through my classes without studying like I had in high school.

"How was Mr. Wonderful?" She giggled as she sat her books down on the desk and then pulled out her pajamas.

"He wants to take me salsa dancing."

"But you don't know how to salsa." She frowned as she pulled off her t-shirt and then slipped on her nightgown.

"I know, but he's taking us to classes."

"Wow." She looked impressed and the fell on top of her bed. "I'm so tired."

"Aww." I gave her a sympathetic look. "You don't have to go hardcore right away."

"I do. I need to get a 4.0 GPA if I want to get into Harvard or Yale Law."

"We just started undergrad, Meg." I giggled.

"I know that. You know that. But does Brandon Hastings know that as yet?"

"No," I groaned and lay staring at the ceiling. "I can't tell him, Meg. Not yet. He won't want to see me if he knows I'm eighteen."

"You never know."

"Trust me, I know. He's working on Wall Street, living in a swanky apartment, and I've just started college living in the dorms with a roommate in single beds." My stomach tightened in knots. "He wouldn't give me the time of day if he knew."

"You're still you. He'll still like you."

"No, he won't. He'll think I'm a kid."

"I don't know, Katie. I just have a bad feeling he's going to figure out you're not twenty-two."

"I'll tell him eventually," I sighed. "Once we get to

know each other better. I'll tell him then."

"Okay." She yawned. "Shit, I'm tired. I'm falling asleep already."

"Sweet dreams, Meg."

And in response, she started snoring.

The next day was crazy. Meg lent me one of her dresses and another pair of heels, and I walked to the station on 116th with a huge grin on my face. I knew I looked good because I had caught several guys eyeing me as I walked down Broadway. I was so excited I thought I was going to throw up. I was going on a date with a hot man—a very hot man—and all I wanted to do was sing and smile. I changed trains in Herald Square and then looked on my phone for the best directions to get to the restaurant. I got a little lost and ended up arriving about ten minutes late. I saw Brandon waiting outside for me and his eyes lit up as I ran over to him quickly.

"Sorry," I gasped, slightly out of breath. "I can't walk fast in these heels."

"You should have caught a cab."

"I, uh, prefer the train. It's more environmentally friendly," I lied. I only had a thousand dollars to last me a few months and I certainly wasn't going to waste it on cabs.

"I do like a girl that thinks of the environment."

"That's me."

"I thought you were going to stand me up." His blue eyes sparkled as he surveyed my appearance. I looked him over hungrily. He looked even more handsome than I had remembered, with a crisp light blue shirt that illuminated his eyes and a pair of grey slacks. He had on flat black leather shoes that looked expensive and shiny.

"Oh, sorry. I got a little lost." I made a face and he laughed before reaching over and kissed me lightly. I stood there looking at him stupidly, and he laughed and ran his hands through his hair.

"Sorry, I've been waiting to kiss you for a week."

16

"No need to apologize. I liked it."

"You're always so honest. I love it."

"I try." I smiled back weakly, thinking about the big lie I was keeping from him.

"We can skip dinner if you want." He leaned in toward me and I could feel the warmth of his skin even though he wasn't touching me.

"Oh? You want to go straight to the salsa classes?" I asked stupidly.

"No, I was thinking we could go back to my place."

"Your place?" I stared at him for a moment before it clicked. "Oh. Oh." I blushed and bit my lower lip as I wondered what to say. "I don't have sex on the first date," I finally blurted out. "I'm not a prude or anything, but I've always thought that—"

"No need to explain." He grabbed my hand. "I respect your want to wait. It will make it more special."

"Exactly." I nodded in agreement and walked with him into the restaurant.

"How was work today, Katie?"

"Uh, pretty good. You?"

"It was the same. Only it wasn't as bad, as I knew I was going to see you this evening."

"That's sweet." I blushed. "I thought about you today as well."

"I guess that's a sign."

"Sign of what?"

"That we're meant to be." He winked at me and I felt my heart explode in happiness. This was a man who knew how to worm his way into a woman's heart.

***

"Ladies and gentlemen, we're approaching San Francisco International Airport. We should be landing in about thirty minutes. Please put your seats in the upright position." The captain's words diverted me from my memories again. I made sure my seat was upright and my seatbelt tightened as I smiled at the memories of that first weekend. I had stayed the whole weekend at Brandon's apartment and we had stayed up all of Friday night watching French movies on Netflix. Then on Saturday he had taken me into Brooklyn and we'd had brunch at a cute little place in Park Slope. It had been perfect. He hadn't even tried to touch me. Just two long, intense kisses before bed and then he'd fallen asleep while I lay there staring at his back, wanting to touch him and feel his skin next to mine. Only I'd been too scared and pathetic. I'd still been a girl pretending to be a woman.

CHAPTER 2

"Welcome to the Diva Hotel, Mrs. Raymond."

"Ms." I smiled at the front desk clerk. "It's Ms."

"Sorry, Ms. Raymond. Would you prefer two full size beds or one king?"

"King, please." I handed her my credit card for incidentals and waited for my room key.

"Is there anything else we can help you with today?"

"No, that's all, thanks." I took my credit card back, grabbed my suitcase, and walked over to the elevator. I saw a doorway to my left that led to a Starbucks, and I figured I could grab a coffee there in the morning before the orientation started. I was going to need to be as alert as possible as soon as I arrived. I walked into the elevator with its fluorescent purple lights and was immediately taken back to the night I had convinced Brandon to go to a nightclub with me. It had been the second week we had been seeing each other. We'd gone out to dinner and were walking back to his place when we passed Doug's. I'd grabbed his arm and stopped him.

"Let's go in." I grinned and nodded toward the door. The strobe lights and booming top-40 music crept through the doorway and he shuddered. "Come on, it'll be fun."

"I don't do clubs." He shook his head with a small smile.

"Just for five minutes."

"I guess I could do five minutes." He grabbed my hand and we walked in easily without being carded, just as I thought. I wasn't dumb this time, and we bypassed the bar, going straight to the dance floor. I grabbed his hands and started dancing. At first, he was a bit stiff. I could tell that he wasn't one for bumping and grinding, but he seemed to get into the swing of things very quickly. One of my favorite rap songs came on, and I pushed back against him excitedly. He seemed to enjoy it and allowed his hands to roam freely over my stomach and all the way up to the underside of my breasts as he held on to me.

I could remember the next moment clearly. A purple strobe light illuminated us in the room and we danced slowly in the crowd of people. I laughed and shimmied, enjoying the vitality I felt in the room. Then his hands slid all the way up, and I felt them cupping my breasts as we danced. I paused for a split second, startled by the feel of his hands kneading my breasts. It felt different and it felt good. I looked around quickly to see if anyone had noticed, but no one was paying attention to us. They were too caught up in what they were doing.

Doug's was filled with people, but in that moment, as the beat ruined our hearing and our bodies moved together as one, it felt like we were all alone and my body felt like it was on fire. His fingers became more aggressive against my breasts, and as he pinched my nipples, I backed into him hard, crying out in pleasure, though the sound was muffled by the music around us.

Brandon pulled me around and into him, and then his lips came crashing down on mine. I kissed him back eagerly, my tongue entering his mouth and exploring every part. I sucked on his tongue eagerly, enjoying the faint taste of chocolate from the shared dessert we'd had at the restaurant. His hands lowered from my back to my ass, and he cupped my ass cheeks as he pushed me into him. I gasped against his mouth as I felt something hard pressing against my belly. I knew without a doubt that it was his erection, and a secret thrill ran from the tips of my toes, up my legs, through my belly, to my tingling breasts, and into my eager mouth. I had done that to him. I had turned him on and he wanted me. It made me feel heady with power. Here was this handsome, rich, and captivating man, and he wanted me. Even though I didn't have a lot of experience and I didn't dress in fancy clothes or know how to apply makeup. Even though I talked about movies too much and rambled on about poets and writers late into the night. He still wanted me.

I kissed him back harder then, pushing myself into him, running my hands through his hair. I was caught up in the moment as I ravished him harder than he'd ravished me. Sometimes I thought that if he had wanted to, I would have even let him make love to me right there on the dance floor.

"Now, now, Katie." He pulled away from me with lust-filled eyes. "This isn't the place."

"Let's go then." I grabbed his hand without thinking and pulled him off of the dance floor. "Let's go back to your place." His eyes grew dark with desire at my words as he pushed me against the wall and ran his fingers down my neck. He stared into my eyes with such intensity that it was all I could do to not reach over and touch him.

"Are you sure you want to do that?" He growled into my ear. "Because if I take you tonight, there will be no letting go. No turning back. I will make you mine. I will possess you."

"I want you to take me." I swallowed hard at his words.

"I want you so bad, Katie." He shook his head as if to clear his mind. "Ever since the morning after I took you home, I've wanted you."

"So then take me."

"We don't have to do this if you're not ready."

I laughed then. Big, happy, and immature laughs. "Of course I'm ready. I've practically been begging you for the last ten minutes."

"Then let's go." He grabbed my hand and pulled me out of the club. We ran like school kids down the road to his apartment. Both of us aching to touch and be touched by each other. It was only when we got to his apartment door that I really stopped to think about what I was about to do. I was about to lose my virginity to a guy I had known for two weeks. Was I a slut? Was I doing the right thing? But my thoughts quickly dissipated as he picked me up, carried me into the apartment, and plopped me down on the bed.

"Would you like some wine or champagne?" He grinned down at me, and he looked like a wolf as I stared up at him. A sexy, devilish, and powerful wolf. I shook my head slowly and stared up at him, wondering if I should tell him this was my first time. It took me all of three seconds to shoot down the idea. I knew he thought I was quaint and that I wasn't used to big city ways because I was from a small town in Florida, but I knew it wouldn't be as believable that I was a virgin. I couldn't imagine he came across many twenty-two-year-old virgins.

He started to unbutton his shirt and I stared up at him with desire pouring out of every part of my body. I gazed up at him in admiration as he threw his shirt onto the floor. His chest was well-built, with a small spattering of hair, and his six-pack looked like something from a fitness magazine. He fell down onto the bed to me, and I reached over and lightly ran my fingers along his chest, grazing his nipples. He gasped at my touch and rolled over on top of me.

"You're wearing too many clothes," he growled, his eyes dark and intense. "Sit up." He pulled me up and I lifted my hands up so that he could pull my top off. His fingers gently went to my back and unclasped my bra before he threw it onto the floor along with my top. "Oh, Katie," he groaned before pushing me back onto the bed. His lips immediately fell to my right breast as his fingers played with my left one. I gasped as he took my nipple in his mouth and gently nibbled on it as he sucked. He sucked as if his life depended on it, and I felt my body trembling underneath him as moisture filled my panties. I reached my hands around to his back and ran my fingers up and down, squeezing his shoulders tightly as his lips moved away from my right breast. I moaned as his lips clasped down on my left breast and my legs reached up to encircle him.

"Oh, Katie," he moaned again as he kissed up my chest and neck and back to my lips. "You taste so sweet," he muttered against my lips as his tongue found sanctuary in my mouth again. "Do you taste as sweet everywhere?"

"Everywhere?" I answered him, not thinking. All I wanted to do was feel him against me, inside of me. My body had never felt so alive before.

"Hmm, yes, everywhere." His lips left mine as he kissed back down my body, stopping at the top of my jeans for a few moments as his hands undid the button and pulled them off of me. I lay there in just my panties gazing up at him, not sure what he was going to do next. I didn't have to wait long to find out. His fingers traced an invisible line up my leg and only stopped once they reached my panties. I held my breath as his fingers ran right down the middle of my panties and circled me. I gasped and squirmed on the bed as he teased me.

"Please, Brandon," I groaned. I wanted—no I needed—to feel more of him. I needed to feel him closer, his skin against mine.

"Shh." He smiled at me and slipped his fingers into the side of my panties and rubbed my wetness. "Oh, Katie," he groaned as I continued squirming. "You are so wet for me."

"I want you," I groaned as I reached up to him, wanting to feel his chest against mine. "Let me touch you."

"Not yet." He slipped his fingers out of my panties and then pulled them down slowly and agonizingly. Every second felt like an eternity, and all I wanted was to feel his warmth against me again. I cried out when he lowered his mouth to my pussy and sucked on my bud. And then I screamed when his tongue entered me, slowly and deeply, pushing me to cliffs I never knew had existed. My fingers grabbed the sheets as his tongue continued to enter me, and I felt like I was going to die of pleasure. Waves of ecstasy took over my body so that all I could think about was the pleasure rolling through my body. "Come for me, Katie," he muttered against my pussy, and the feel of his breath against me was another new and exciting sensation. "Come for me."

"I-I can't," I groaned, shaking my head. I had never felt this way before and I was afraid that my bladder was going to burst if he kept on. "Please." I groaned as his hands spread my legs wider and he licked and sucked me with more intensity.

This time when his tongue entered me, I couldn't control it, and my orgasm exploded, sending ripple effects down my body.

"Oh, Brandon!" I screamed as my body trembled under him. He continued his exploration and his tongue lapped me up eagerly before he returned back up to kiss me.

"You taste even sweeter down there." He grinned at me before his mouth descended onto mine again. I could taste myself on his lips, and I moaned as his fingers worked their way back down my stomach and to my sweet spot. I reached my hands down to his slacks, wanting to pull them down and touch him. He laughed as I fumbled around with his button, jumped up, and pulled them off along with his boxers.

I stared at him in amazement. His cock looked like a warrior—thick, strong and firm. I swallowed as I imagined it inside of me. He looked bigger than I had imagined from photos I'd seen online with friends. I reached over and touched him softly, and he groaned as my fingers slowly worked their way up and down his shaft. I squeezed the tip of his cock and he pushed me back down on the bed.

"If you keep teasing me, Katie, I'm going to come a lot faster than I want for our first time together."

"I don't mind." I shook my head and giggled as he growled against my neck.

"I'm going to make you forget all your other lovers. I'm going to make sure that mine is the only face you think of when you think of making love. I want your body to remember me and only me."

"Okay," I gasped and closed my eyes as his fingers played with me again and his tongue tasted the lines of my neck. My hands grabbed his ass and I tried to push him toward me so that I could feel him against me.

"Oh, Katie. I need to enter you," he groaned against me ear. "Tell me you're on the pill."

"No." My eyes popped up and I bit my lower lip. "I'm not, uh, on the pill."

"Damn." He looked upset as he got off of the bed. "I wanted to feel all of you. I wanted to feel your skin against my skin, but it's fine. I have some condoms."

"Oh." I watched as he opened the drawer on his nightstand and pulled out a big box. "Did you get them because of me?"

"No." He chuckled as he pulled two out and placed one on the top of the stand. "I make sure to keep a supply."

"Oh." I looked away from him, jealousy filling me.

"You're not upset, are you?" His eyes peered at me. "You can't think I don't have sex?"

"I didn't know you were sleeping around."

"I haven't slept with anyone since I've met you."

"That was two weeks ago."

"I'm not a monk, Katie." He sat on the bed. "I like sex. We're adults. It's not a crime."

"I know." I nodded.

"If it makes you feel better, I don't want to sleep with

anyone else." He smiled and kissed me hard. "I know we've only been seeing each other for two weeks, but let's see how it goes. I think we could have something special."

"Okay." I nodded again, feeling slightly happier.

"So we agree not to sleep with anyone else, right?"

"Right." I nodded a third time and he kissed me hard.

He ripped open the condom packet and quickly slid it onto his cock before lowering himself down onto me, allowing his chest to crush down on my breasts.

"Wrap your legs around my waist," he commanded me and I did so eagerly. I felt the tip of his cock at my entrance and gasped, waiting for him to finally enter me. "Oh, God, you're so wet," he groaned as he slowly entered me. I felt myself contract against him as he entered me, and for one brief second, I was scared that it was going to hurt. "Oh, Katie," he groaned as he started moving his body slowly. His cock pushed into me hard and I cried out as I felt a brief shot of pain. He looked at me with a confused and dazed look in his eyes, so I closed mine and moved underneath him.

"Fuck me, Brandon!" I cried out, and he continued moving and increasing his speed until he was sliding in and out of me smoothly. I held on to him tightly as our bodies danced to their own rhythm. My breasts bounced against his chest and his hands clasped mine as he continued making my body his.

"Open your eyes." His voice was commanding, and I opened them slowly and saw him staring into mine. "I want to see your expression as we come together." He continued moving against me and I felt like I was about to explode when his body started shuddering and he groaned out. I climaxed then, and I held him tight to me as our bodies quaked together before he fell down on top of me. He rolled over to the right and gave me a lazy smile after a few minutes.

"That was amazing." His fingers traced the lines around my nipples as he slowly withdrew his cock from me and slipped the condom off. "Are you a virgin, Katie?" He looked up at me slowly, a question in his eyes.

"No." I shook my head.

"Really? I could have sworn you were a virgin by the way you reacted when I entered you, and I felt like I was breaking through your hymen."

"You asked if I am, but I'm not any longer." I smiled up at him and leaned over to kiss his lips. My body was tired and satiated and there was nothing that was going to ruin this moment for me.

"Ah, you tricky girl." He laughed and then sighed as he pulled me toward him. "Why didn't you tell me?"

"I didn't want you to think I was." I bit my lip.

"Oh, Katie," he whispered against my hair. "Thank you for allowing me to make love to you. I hope it was all you had hoped for."

"It was better than I had hoped for," I mumbled, and his eyes lit up with pride as he lay back with me cuddled into him.

"I'm so glad that I met you, Katie Raymond."

"Me too, Brandon Hastings." I kissed his chest and we both fell asleep.

"Excuse me, ma'am, are you lost?" The front desk clerk walked toward the elevator and stared at me.

"Sorry, what?"

"It's just that you've ridden up and down in the elevator for the last ten minutes."

"Oh, sorry." I blushed. "The purple lights just made me remember something."

"Okay." The lady gave me a strange look. "You're on the sixth floor, if you forgot."

"Yeah, thanks." I pressed the button again and shook my head. "Focus, Katie, focus," I mumbled to myself. Now was not the time to relive my memories of Brandon Hastings. He hated me and I hated him, and I was praying that if he saw me he wouldn't remember who I was. It didn't matter how great it had been when we first started dating. It didn't matter that his touch made my whole body melt. It was over. He had broken my heart, and if I wasn't careful, he was going to ruin my business career as well.

I walked out of the purple-lit elevator and to my room reluctantly. I didn't want to be here. I didn't want to be reminded of Brandon. Not now. Not when everything in my life was finally getting better. I had even started dating a new guy just before I got the job. He was a nice guy as well. Matt was someone I could see myself with in a serious relationship. He was safe and I knew he really liked me; it didn't matter that he didn't set my heart on fire like Brandon had. I was older and wiser now. I knew what real love was. What Brandon and I'd had was a fantasy—a fantasy built on lies—and when it all came crashing down, it had nearly broken me. I wasn't going to let myself dwell on the past. I couldn't allow myself to go down that road again.

***

The alarm went off at five a.m. and I wanted to roll over and go back to sleep again. "Get up, Katie," I lectured myself as I pulled the blankets up over me. I groaned and sat up, adjusting my eyes to the darkness.

I got out of bed and turned on the light and opened my suitcase. Meg and I had gone shopping before the trip, and I had gotten the sexiest business attire I could find. I had also gotten some new makeup, new perfume, and a new Chi straightener so that my hair would be as sleek as possible. I wanted to make sure I looked as good as I had ever looked. I didn't want him to recognize me, but if he did, I wanted to look as hot and sexy as possible.

I grabbed my shower cap and walked to the bathroom. I needed to shower first, and then I would do my hair. I stared at my wild waves in the bathroom mirror and groaned. It was going to take at least an hour to get my hair anything close to straight and sleek. I stared at my appearance again and started laughing as I thought about going to work looking like this. Brandon would definitely remember me if I turned up like this.

***

"Let's shower together." Brandon pulled me out of bed with him the night after we made love for the first time.

"I'm still tired," I mumbled.

"There's time to sleep tonight."

"Not if you wake me up a million times tonight like you did last night."

"Well, I need to get as much of you as I can while you're here."

"I'll be here next weekend." I yawned and stretched.

"I'd love it if you stayed here this week as well."

"What?" I froze and looked at him with wide eyes.

"I know, I know. I'm moving too fast. Sorry, I've just never felt this way before."

"Oh." I jumped out of bed and kissed him. "I've never felt this way before either."

"I just want to spend every night with you."

"I know." I sighed. "But I need to stay at my own place. It's just easier for me to get to work from there."

"I guess I could spend a couple of nights there if you want."

"No!" I shouted and then stepped back. "Sorry, it's a mess and I'd be embarrassed for you to see it."

"Don't be embarrassed." He pulled me toward him and kissed me. "I'm sure you have lots of debt from college, and I'm sure your new job can't be paying you that much. I don't care where you live."

"Uh, thanks." I buried my face into his chest, shame turning my face red. "It's hard as a new grad, you know, especially in this economy."

"Where did you go to school again?" He questioned

me.

"Columbia... Uh, I mean, I always wanted to go to Columbia. I went to Florida Atlantic University," I mumbled, wanting to die.

"I'm always looking for new account managers for the hedge fund, if you're interested in doing stocks?"

"Oh, thanks, but I couldn't." I smiled weakly. "It wouldn't be right. We only just started dating. I don't want you to think I'm taking advantage of you."

"I know." He kissed the top of my head. "I think that's why I like you so much. You're the furthest thing from a gold digger I've met in New York."

"Well, you would know," I said, quite surly, and he laughed.

"Don't be jealous, Katie."

"I'm not," I pouted and followed him into the bathroom. "Oh my God, look at my hair!" I cried out as I looked into the mirror and saw a crazy mess. "I look awful."

"No, you don't. You look beautiful." He walked up behind me and put his arms around my waist. "Though I can check to see if there are any lost birds."

"Lost birds?" I wiggled against him as I looked back at him.

"You know, that thought your hair was a nest."

"Jerk." I laughed as he picked me up and placed me on the vanity.

"I can be a jerk if you want."

"Oh?" I pulled him toward me and felt his hardening cock against my leg.

"Yeah, I can do this." He placed the tip of his cock against my pussy and pushed it in slightly so that the tip was inside me. "And I can do this." He slowly entered me and I moaned as I felt him inside me. "And then I can do this." He withdrew from me and I whimpered as he left my body.

"Brandon," I groaned and he laughed.

"I told you I can be a jerk."

I squeezed my legs around him and tried to pull him into me again but he laughed.

"Not so fast, young lady."

"Make love to me," I groaned as I reached up to kiss him.

"I don't have a condom on me." He shrugged and I let out a light groan, disappointed. "You should get on the pill."

"Huh?" I bit down into his shoulder, distracted by his musk.

"You should go to the doctor and get on the pill."

"Oh, okay," I murmured as I ran my fingers down his abs.

"Do you have health insurance at your job? Do you need me to take you to my doctor?"

"I have health insurance." I licked down his chest as he fondled my breasts. "I'll go in on Monday." I would have to look online to see what time the university health center opened. I cringed as I thought about having to tell the nurse why I was there. But I figured they should be happy I was having safe sex. This wasn't my high school anymore. I wasn't going to get a lecture about abstinence.

"I wish you were on it now," he whispered in my ear. "I want to take you right here and feel your pussy walls close in on my cock as I take you on a journey you've never even imagined."

"So why don't you?" I gasped, willing him to enter me.

"I don't want to get you pregnant." He chuckled and stared at me seriously. "I'm not really a guy that's done relationships, and this is new to me. I don't want to mess anything up."

"You won't." I took his face in my hands and kissed him softly. "You won't mess anything up," I whispered against my lips and my heart fluttered as he carried me back to the bedroom and to his bed.

I had been right as well. He hadn't messed anything up.

I had.

***

Fisherman's Wharf was not full of fishermen. Or at least it wasn't when I arrived. I walked around for a little bit, glad that it wasn't hot and humid. Hot and humid meant my perfectly coiffed hair would be a frizzy mess in minutes.

Once it hit eight a.m., I walked into the building that Marathon Corps's company-wide orientation was going to be in and looked around for a welcome table. I saw it right away, and I gasped as I walked toward it. The table was decorated with white orchids, and I couldn't not think of the night I'd realized that I'd loved him. Every time I saw orchids, I thought of Brandon. Even Meg knew never to bring them into the apartment we shared. Every time I saw them, I cried. Even now, I felt teary eyed. I took a deep breath and continued toward the table. I couldn't afford to get emotional now. Not now. Not when my makeup looked so perfect. It didn't matter that my heart was beating in my stomach and all my senses were in high alert. It didn't matter that there were orchids there. It meant nothing, absolutely nothing.

Brandon and I had seen each other every weekend for the first two months of our dating. He had asked to come over to my apartment several times but seemed to accept the fact that I'd been too embarrassed to have him in my apartment. We saw each other some weeknights as well, but he seemed to like the fact that I didn't ask to see him every day. I gave him his space. I didn't call or text him every few hours, and I didn't check up on him. He didn't know that I didn't have time to check on him. I was in classes or the library most days, and phones were banned from both. I had to study in the daytime because I knew I wouldn't have any time on the weekends and rarely in the evenings. He just thought I was comfortable and secure in the relationship. I was too naïve to even think that there was anything to worry about. To me, he was just Brandon, a handsome man I was dating, but to the rest of New York, he was one of the most eligible bachelors in the city.

"Can you come over tonight?" I glanced at the text as I walked to my next class. It was a Wednesday, and I had an English test the next day.

"I think so," I texted back quickly and happily.

"Can you take the day off of work tomorrow?"

"Don't think so. You know Maggie," I texted back quickly. Maggie was my fictional boss. Meg and I had spent an entire night creating a fake company and job for me. Maggie was my bitch of a boss who hated me and made me work late a lot.

"I wish you would quit that job and come and work for me. ;) ;)" I laughed at his text.

"You know we wouldn't get much work done."

"I want you right now," he texted back. "I want to bend you over my desk and take you right now."

"Maybe one day."

"Shit, I'm going to have to lock my door."

"Uh oh, why?"

"I'm going to have to take care of business and I don't want my secretary to walk in."

"Wish I was there."

"So do I. So can you come over tonight?"

"I'll try to get out of work early." I bit my lip as I typed that. I knew that I needed to study, but I really wanted to see him as well.

"Great. I'll see you at 6. Don't eat. We can get take out."

"Okay, see you at 6." I hurried into the class, looked down at my jeans and t-shirt, and sighed. I'd have to go home, change into some more professional clothes, and then hurry to catch the train by five. There would be no time for me to try and study for an hour before I left.

I arrived at Brandon's place at about 6:30 p.m. and he

pulled me into his arms as soon as he opened the door.

"I missed you." He kissed me and stared at my face.

"You saw me on Sunday."

"That was too long ago."

"Oh, Brandon." I squeezed his hand and walked into the apartment.

"I want you to move in with me." He grabbed me from behind and pulled me toward him again. "I want you to wake up next to me every morning."

"I told you, I can't. I have a lease." I giggled as he kissed my neck.

"I'll pay the lease off," he groaned and then walked away and into the kitchen. "I have something for you." He walked back toward me with an orchid plant.

"What's this?"

"It's an orchid plant."

"Thank you." I smiled and took it from him. "It's beautiful."

"Where would you like to put it?"

"Huh?"

"It's your housewarming gift."

"Housewarming?"

"This is your new home."

"But—"

"But nothing." He shook his head seriously. "I told you the night we made love that you're mine now."

"I..." I swallowed hard, feeling the intensity of his emotions reverberating off of his body.

"You're the only woman I've ever asked to live with me." He grabbed my hands. "I thought you'd be happy."

"I am. It just seems so fast."

"Is it my age?" He sighed and my heart quickened.

"What?" I stammered. Did he know?

"I know I'm thirty-five and you're in your early twenties. I know there is more of the world you want to see and explore. I don't want to be selfish, but you're special. You're someone I could spend the rest of my life with."

"Do you think I'm too young for you?" I bit my lip and he laughed.

"If anyone would have asked me how young I would date, I never would have said twenty-two before I met you."

"Oh." I smiled weakly. "And now?"

"And now, I don't think age matters."

"So you'd date someone younger than twenty-two?"

"Oh, hell no." He laughed. "I have a reputation. I'd have nothing in common with someone younger."

"I see."

"So you're mine now, Katie." He gazed deep into my eyes. "Move in with me and let me spoil you." I kissed him then because I didn't know what to say. How could I tell him that I lived in a dorm on campus? How could I tell him that I was eighteen and that there was no way in hell my parents would approve of me cohabitating with a man almost twice my age? A man who had taken my virginity. A man they had never met!

"So, where shall we put the orchid?"

"In the kitchen, by the window." I pulled away from him slowly. "They like light."

"Good idea." He reached into his pocket and smiled at me. "I have something else for you."

My face went white as I saw him pulling his hand out... *Oh God*, I thought, *he's going to propose.*

"Here is a set of keys."

"Keys?" I looked at him blankly and then laughed as I realized what they were for. "Oh, thank you."

"Now, let's go to bed."

"To bed?"

"I need to have you now. I've been dreaming of making love to you since you left."

"Oh, I thought we were going to eat?"

"You want to eat?" He looked incredulous.

"I'm a bit hungry." I nodded and then my stomach

growled. His eyes crinkled and he laughed heartily before he grabbed me up and swung me around.

"Then eat you shall." He kissed my forehead and put me back down. "I love you, Katie," he whispered into my ear. I melted against him and passionately kissed him back. It was the first time he had said those words to me, and it gave me a heady feeling. I stared at the orchids and smiled as his hands rubbed my back. The orchids signaled a change in our relationship—a change I was excited about, even if I wasn't quite sure how everything was going to work out.

"Are you here for the orientation?" a sharp voice questioned me, and I looked up with a tight smile.

"Yes, I am. Katie Raymond from the New York office."

"Okay, let me find your packet." The lady looked back at me with glassy blue eyes, her red hair cut in a sharp bob. She had a nametag on that read Priscilla and I thought the name suited her. A bitchy name for a bitchy-looking person.

"Here." She roughly handed me a folder. "Walk down the hallway to the elevator, go up to the tenth floor, and get out. You'll see the signs to show you to your first meeting."

"Thanks," I nodded and was about to say more, but she was already speaking to the person behind me. I walked to the elevator uncertainly, feeling out of place. I didn't fit in here. Sometimes I wondered if I was cut out for the business world.

I waited a few minutes for the elevator and walked in slowly. Part of me wanted to run out, catch a plane back home, and just look for another job. I didn't even bother looking up when the elevator stopped at the next floor.

I was debating whether I should just go home when I realized that whoever had entered the elevator hadn't pressed a button. It was then that I looked up. It was then that my life flashed before my eyes. I fell back against the wall as I stared into his face. He looked different, but he also looked the same. Everything about this moment was so much worse and so much more powerful than I had imagined it would be.

"Hello, Katie."

"Hello, Brandon," I whispered and stared at his face, trying to memorize every line and hair for future reference. He took a step toward me, and his hands rested on my shoulders. I swallowed hard and looked up so that our eyes were connected. Then he leaned in and pressed his lips against mine softly.

"That's for the memories," he whispered, and I smiled at him weakly, tears filling my eyes. I couldn't believe he'd remembered that line. It had been so many years since he'd first said it.

CHAPTER 3

"That's for the memories." Brandon pushed me against the elevator wall as soon as the door closed.

"What memories?" I stared at him, wide-eyed.

"The ones we're about to make."

"Huh?"

"Shh!" He placed a finger against my lips. "If you make noise, people may hear."

"Hear what?" I stared at the glint in his eyes. "Brandon, what are you thinking?"

"You know how I've always dreamed of office sex?"

"Uh huh."

"So, we're about to have some."

"We're not in the office." I shook my head and then his meaning dawned on me. "What if someone comes in?" I looked at the doorway in a panic.

"No one will come in." He grinned. "I put a sign on the doors, and we're stopped right now."

"Oh my God, Brandon." My face went bright red. "I don't know about this."

"I'm a bad influence, aren't I?" He bent down and sucked on my neck. "But I just want to have you everywhere."

"You can have me everywhere in the apartment." I laughed. "Everywhere and anywhere."

"Now that we live together, that's not so much fun." His fingers ran up my shirt. "That's safe sex."

"I thought you were all about safe sex." I raised an eyebrow at him and he growled as his fingers slipped under my bra and squeezed my nipples. "Oh," I moaned.

"You know you want to." He unbuttoned my shirt, bent his head, and took my nipple in his mouth.

"Oh, Brandon," I moaned and my hands squeezed his arm muscles. "How can I say no?"

"You can't. You're just as insatiable as I am," he growled as his hand slipped in between my legs. "I'm glad you wore a skirt today."

"You chose my outfit." I rolled my eyes at him.

"Well, I wanted to see you in your new skirt."

"Uh huh."

"And your new thong." He licked his lips and I laughed, not quite believing how different my life was right now. I had been 'living' with Brandon now for two weeks and it was working out quite well. We had a rule where we kept work at work, so I didn't have to discuss what was going on in the *office* if I didn't want to. Brandon had been aghast when I had moved in with one lonely suitcase. I'd made some excuse up about my not having much stuff, which was true—all the furniture belonged to Columbia University. He'd felt so bad for me that he had taken me shopping and showered me with clothes and underwear. I felt a bit like Julia Roberts in *Pretty Woman*, only I didn't mind. He was my boyfriend, not my john, and he loved me. It was all okay if he loved me.

I mean, I could see it in his eyes and hear it in his voice. I'd never felt so special before, so loved. It almost made me wonder why I had put so much time and effort into my studies in high school when I could have been dating and having fun. Wasn't this what life was about? Living and feeling? Not just reading and researching all day. Though I knew Meg and the others were deeply concerned about the direction in which my life was going.

"It's not a good idea, Katie." Meg had begged me to rethink moving in with Brandon.

"I'll still be your roommate too, technically." I'd sighed. "Don't worry. You'll still see me all the time."

"I don't know, Katie."

"He's a nice guy, Meg."

"Well, I've never met him, so how would I know?" I'd left then, because what could I say? She knew why she had never met him. All of my friends knew why. I wasn't a liar. Well, only with him.

"You're wet already," he growled as his fingers slipped between my legs.

"Well, how can I not be?" I pushed him back into the side panel of the elevator and kissed him hard. He groaned as my hands fell to his belt buckle and undid it smoothly. I was now a pro at getting him undone in record time.

"I love it when you take charge."

"I love it when you want us to make memories," I laughed as I unzipped him and kissed my way down his shirt before falling onto my knees and taking him into my mouth. I felt heady with power as he groaned and pulled my hair as I bobbed up and down on him. The salty taste of him growing in my mouth turned me on even more and I took him into my mouth faster and more eagerly.

"Slow down, Katie," Brandon groaned. "I'm going to come if you keep this up."

"That's the idea." I laughed and took him into my mouth as far as I could go. Brandon was the first and only man I'd ever given a blowjob. He was the first of many things. He only knew about the sex though. I wasn't sure how he'd feel if he knew just how inexperienced I had been previous to meeting him. I tried to blank that out of my mind, though the guilt was making everything harder and harder.

He called out my name as he orgasmed into my mouth. I swallowed without thinking, wanting to taste all of him, enjoying the feel of his release as it smoothly slid down my throat.

"Oh how I love you, Katie." He pulled me up and turned me around, bending me over and pushing my thong to the side as his fingers slowly entered me. "Oh, you're so ready for me." He grunted as his fingers roughly made love to me. "I can never get enough of you." He groaned and removed his fingers quickly. I moaned in response, and before I knew it, he was sliding into me fast and deep.

"You're hard again already?" I cried out in surprise and gratification.

"I just have to look at you to be hard, Katie." He grunted as he held on to my hips. His hands swung me around and reached up to squeeze my breasts. "Hold on to the wall. I don't want you to fall."

"Fall?" I questioned between gasps, but I soon realized what he was talking about as he slid in and out of me with such force and intensity that I could barely stand still. "Oh Brandon!" I screamed as his cock fell out of me. "Don't stop."

"I'm not going to." His cock entered me again, and this time he moved in and out so slowly that I thought time was standing still. My nerve endings felt like they were going to explode, and I wiggled my ass to try and get him to move faster again. I needed to feel him deep inside of me. I needed him to consume and take me. I needed to have him possess every inch of my body and soul.

I gripped the wall and closed my eyes as he took me in the elevator. I screamed as he increased his pace and my body started trembling as my orgasm built up.

"Come for me, Katie," he groaned. "Come for me."

"I'm close," I whimpered. My hips buckled underneath him as his fingers reached around and played with my clit while he continued his dominance over my body. "Oh Brandon!" I screamed." I'm coming, I'm coming." I screamed as my body shuddered and he continued fucking me. I banged my hands against the wall and hit something.

Before I knew what was happening, the elevator started moving.

"Oh shit, Katie. What did you do?" he groaned as he continued sliding in and out of me.

"I don't know!" I screamed again as the orgasm took over my body. I couldn't think about anything other than the pleasure that was reverberating through me. "Oh, Brandon, I love you!" I cried out in ecstasy. And then the elevator stopped. What happened next was most probably one of the most exciting, exhilarating, and scary parts of my life. Brandon grabbed me and pulled me to the corner of the elevator with him. He pushed the front of my skirt down and handed me his briefcase to hold. Seconds later, the door opened and two men walked in.

"Good afternoon, Mr. Hastings." They nodded and smiled at him.

"Mark. Jason." He smiled at them before they pressed their floor buttons and faced the front.

"Don't say a word," Brandon whispered in my ear. I stifled a gasp as I felt him push me forward slightly and slip his cock back inside of me. He moved slowly, not wanting to draw any attention to us.

"What are you doing?" I gasped as I whispered back to him.

"I'm going to come again." He winked at me. "And I think we'd all I rather come in you than in my hands and on the floor."

"Oh, Brandon." I shook my head.

"Just move back a little bit to meet me," he whispered. "Yes, keep moving your hips like that. Oh yes." His fingers dug into my hips, and I pretended to stare at something on the ground as I felt his body trembling behind me.

One of the men turned around. "You heard Pepsi shot up two hundred points, right, Brandon?"

"Yeah." His voice was rough, and I smiled.

"Your dad was happy, said if it keeps up we'll all have

big bonuses this year."

"That would be nice," Brandon grunted as his fingers tightened their grip. A devious thought crossed my mind and I started humming and gyrating.

"What are you doing?" Brandon asked casually as the guy stared at us both.

"Nothing. Just dancing to the music in my head."

"I see." His eyes glinted at me and I smiled at him.

"Do you work here?" The guy gave me a friendly look. "I've never seen you before."

"I'm Katie." I smiled at him and shook his head. "I'm a friend of Brandon's."

"She's my girlfriend," Brandon mumbled, and I noticed the guy's surprised look.

"Oh." He turned back around and Brandon pulled me back so that I was right against him. I felt his body shuddering as his cock slid in and out of me quickly. He let out a slight groan and then I felt an explosion of warm semen fill me up as he orgasmed in me.

"This is our stop. See you later." The guy nodded as they exited the elevator, and neither Brandon nor I responded.

"Do you think they knew?" I gasped as Brandon turned me around and kissed me hard. He brushed the back of my skirt down and quickly zipped up his pants.

"Who knows? Who cares?" He laughed and grabbed my hand.

"I guess not you."

"Why should I care? This is the best elevator ride I've ever had." He laughed and kissed my cheek. "I don't know how I got so lucky."

"I don't know how either," I joked, and his eyes grew serious.

"I think you may very well be the one, Katie Raymond. You may very well be the one."

"So how have you been?" Brandon asked me softly at the same time I mumbled, "Fancy seeing you here." He chuckled and I blushed.

"I'm good. How are you?" I spoke softly, scared that he could hear my rapidly beating heart. My eyes took in his appearance greedily. He looked even more handsome than I remembered, but just as smart in his dark grey suit. His hair looked as black as ever, and it was still moist from his morning shower. He hadn't shaved this morning—I could tell from the light stubble around his chin—and I clenched my hands to stop myself from rubbing my fingers over it. This elevator ride was so much different than the elevator ride we'd had so many years ago.

"Great." He rubbed his lips. "Sorry about the kiss. I forgot for a moment."

"It's fine." I blushed, not needing to ask what he had forgotten.

"You look well." He looked me over quickly and disinterestedly. I felt disappointed that he hadn't studied my body a little longer—or my face—but I guess he just didn't care.

"Thank you. So do you," I spoke disjointedly, and it felt weird being so polite with someone who knew every intimate part of my body

"You still look bright-eyed and bushy-tailed." He smiled at me, but it didn't reach his eyes. "I guess you'll always have a youthful look."

"Yes, I guess so." I turned my face away, heat flooding my face at his unsubtle comments.

"So you work for Marathon Corp?" he asked me casually as we exited the elevator.

"Yes, yes I do."

"I take it the resume wasn't faked?" He raised an eyebrow and I stared at him blankly. This was going to be harder than I thought.

"Everything on my resume was true."

"It's a good thing it's illegal to ask for someone's age

when hiring them, isn't it?" He looked at me coldly and I shivered. All pretense was gone from his demeanor. He still hated me. He still hadn't forgiven me.

"I made a mistake once." I looked him directly in the eye. "I've never done it again."

"That's good to hear. Or is that another lie?"

"I didn't mean to lie." I repeated the words I had cried to him so many times in the past.

"If it had only been one small lie and you had told me the truth, then I would have understood. But you perpetuated a fabrication of your life." He stared at me with a hostile expression as his words tore into my soul. "Everything was a lie."

"It wasn't all a lie." I bit my lip. *I did love you*, I wanted to scream at him. *I did love you and you were supposed to love me. You were supposed to forgive me.* But I kept quiet.

"You'd still be lying if I hadn't caught you." He shook his head furiously. "It was all just a game for you, wasn't it? A high school girl caught up in a high school game."

"I wasn't in high school."

"Close enough." He looked away from me. "What difference does a couple of months make?"

I remained silent, not knowing what to say. He was right, of course. I hadn't known when or how I was going to tell him the truth. Of course I had felt guilty. I'd felt extremely guilty. Especially when he'd asked to meet my friends and family. I pretended I'd fallen out with the girls I'd gone to Doug's with that first night and that I hadn't made any new friends yet. Family had been easy to discuss as they were all in Florida. I'd told him that one day we could make a trip for him to meet them and he had been fine with that.

It had become more difficult when he asked about work, wanting to meet my colleagues and attend one of the many happy hours I'd talked about. I had joined some study groups and told him I was trying to bond with workmates. I'd used sex to shut him up every time he'd brought up the topic.

Aside from that, everything else had been going swimmingly. Neither of us was a great cook, so we had taken a gourmet cooking class together every Saturday morning and cooked dinner for each other every Saturday night before making love for hours on end. I suppose eventually that would have gotten old and we would have wanted to do more than cook and have sex, but we'd still been in the honeymoon phase of our relationship.

It had been easy for me to skip the alcohol questions. I'd told him after the hangover I'd had that first night that I didn't really want to drink much anymore, so I'd only had a few sips of wine when we were at home.

When he asked to see my driver's license picture one day, I'd told him I had lost it on the subway and was going to get a new one when I had more time. It hadn't mattered much, as I didn't drive, and we'd never spoken of it again.

Brandon loved to show me new things in the city. I was his first real girlfriend since he had left college. I tried not to think of that too much, though, as I'd always felt jealous when I thought about his ex-fiancée and the subsequent women he had bedded. I didn't like to think of him with other women. I wanted to be the only one in his life and in his memories. He laughed frequently when I asked him who he loved the most, who he thought of the most, who he wanted to be with the most. He thought it was cute that I had small insecurities about his past. He'd always kiss my forehead and tell me I was the one and only in his life, forever and always, and I would happily melt against him.

Everything was going perfectly, up until that day. I had organized my schedule so well that even I forgot that I was just an eighteen-year-old freshman at Columbia University and not an entry-level associate at a marketing firm in the city.

"I've got a work presentation tomorrow," he groaned one night as I ran my hands down to his boxer shorts. "I'm not even prepared."

"Is that your way of telling me no?" I laughed at him and kissed his nipples. "Are you really telling me no?"

"I know. Call me an old man or something. But I have to go and give a talk and I have nothing ready. I'll have to leave early in the morning to prepare and then catch a train to the Upper West Side."

"Aww." I really wasn't listening. I was too busy trying to entice him. If I'd paid better attention, instinct bells would have gone off when he'd said Upper West Side.

"I can tell that you care." He laughed and pulled me on top of him. "What's your day like tomorrow? Can you get out of work early or meet me for lunch?"

"Hmmm." I rubbed myself back and forth on him as he reached up and grabbed my breasts. "I'm not sure. I think I have a meeting." I gasped as he leaned up, took one of my nipples into his mouth, and sucked. "I can see what I can do," I moaned as I increased my pace as I dry-rubbed him. His cock was hanging out of his boxers and rubbing up against me through my panties.

"I'd love to take you to lunch, maybe even have sex in the bathroom."

"What bathroom?" I gasped as he slipped a finger into my panties and rubbed my clit.

"The restaurant bathroom," he groaned as I rubbed my breasts in his face. "I know how you love public sex."

"You mean you love it." I laughed slightly. "I'm not sure if I can tomorrow, my boss wants to have a lunch meeting with me."

"Oh no." He made a face in sympathy. "I hope everything is okay."

"Yeah, it'll be fine." I gasped as he slipped my panties to the side and guided his cock into me. "Oh, I thought you needed to sleep?"

"I'm never so tired that I can say no when my girl wants to ride me." He held my hips as I slowly bounced up and down on him. "Ride me faster, cowgirl." He moved my hips back and forth and I swiveled on top of him, letting his hard cock slide in and out of me like a bullet.

"Call me if you get out early. Maybe we can do a late lunch," he groaned, and I giggled. It was always funny to me when he tried to hold a conversation during sex.

"Will do," I gasped before I screamed. He flipped me over onto my knees and came up behind me and slipped his cock back inside of me. "Oh my!" I screamed again as he slammed into me hard. I loved it when we did it doggy style because I always seemed to feel every inch of him inside of me, hitting spots I'd never known existed before.

"Or think about quitting and coming to work for me." He grunted behind me. "Or maybe even just quit and we can start a family." His words were low and I froze for a second. I didn't respond because an orgasm took over my body and I was screaming out his name to continue fucking me. He came pretty quickly after me, and I snuggled into his arms as we settled in for sleep. I stroked his chest with my eyes closed and enjoyed the warm feeling of satisfaction that rested in me.

"I wasn't just saying that, you know," he whispered against my hair. "I know we haven't been together long and you've just started your career, but I'd really like to take this to the next level soon. I love you, Katie Raymond." I didn't respond to him and pretended that I had fallen asleep, but my heart couldn't stop pounding at his words. I was hopelessly in love with this man and yet scared at the same time. How could I marry him and have his babies when he didn't know the truth about me? Because I knew one hundred percent that he was the man I wanted to spend my life with.

I met Meg for breakfast before my first class the next day because I had nothing to prepare for class. Some top businessman was coming to give a talk about what it meant to be a leader in the business world. I wasn't really interested in hearing what he had to say, but I was glad that I had a day off from reading for class. I filled Meg in on the happenings of the night before, but she didn't look happy for me.

"Katie, I love you. I really do. You're my best friend and I know you love this man. But he's also the first guy you've ever dated. You're moving way too fast. For all you know, this is puppy love."

"It's not puppy love. I love him." I shook my head and sighed. "You just don't understand."

"Does he even know that you're going home for Christmas break?"

"No." I shook my head. "I'm thinking about calling my parents and telling them I can't come. Brandon wants me to meet his folks."

"Katie, you cannot flake out on your parents. Think how disappointed they will be. Not to mention they will be on the first flight out here, and how are you going to explain that you're now living with your older boyfriend?"

I groaned at her words. I knew she was right. I'd have to come up with an excuse to tell Brandon. Maybe I would tell him that my business lunch was me getting a promotion, but I'd have to travel abroad for the holidays.

"What are you doing?" She frowned as I whipped out my phone.

"How does this sound?" I asked her as I started texting. "Guess what, honey? I think I'm getting a promotion. There is a rumor going around the office that my boss is going to promote me. Only thing is, I may be gone for Christmas. Business travel."

"It sounds long and it sounds like a lie." Meg sighed. "Why don't you just tell him the truth?"

"I can't." I shook my head. "Not yet." I hit send and sat back. "You don't understand, Meg. I want to tell him the truth, but I'm just not sure he will understand."

"If he loves you, he will."

"I know." I closed my eyes. "I'm going to tell him after Christmas, I promise."

"Okay." She looked like she wanted to say more, but she didn't. "Did he respond?"

"Yeah," I smiled. "He said, 'Congrats. Can't wait to hear all about it. Wish me luck this morning. I can't stand having to do this talk. Love, your Brandon.'"

"Well, I guess he fell for it." Meg shook her head. "Let's get to campus. I have class in a few minutes."

"Yeah, me too. Just a boring guest lecture though." I grinned. "Maybe I can get started on my biology homework."

"You're so bad, Katie." Meg laughed at me and I shrugged.

"If I sit in the back, no one will notice what I'm doing."

"Good luck with that." We hugged quickly and then parted ways outside Butler Library.

"See you for study group tomorrow?" She looked at me hopefully and I nodded.

"Of course. I need it or I'm going to fail my finals next week." We both laughed even though my words were true, and I walked to my class absentmindedly. I walked into the classroom and sat in the back row, checking my text messages before turning off my phone and putting it in my bag. I pulled out my biology textbook and started going through the checklist my study group and I had prepared for the final. The teacher started talking and introducing the speaker, but I was so engrossed in one of the charts I was making that I didn't even look up.

"Ms. Raymond, do you have something more important than today's class?" the professor called out to me, and my face went red as I looked up to apologize.

"No, sorry, Professor Wright." I offered him a small smile and then froze as I looked to the right of him. In that moment, I felt a million different emotions coursing through my body. I honestly wanted to die or faint, but neither one of them occurred.

The smile left my face as I stared at the guest speaker. It was Brandon, and as his eyes met mine, I saw a flash of surprise, wonder, and anger in his eyes. He looked at me blankly for a moment and I offered him a small smile. He turned away from me and my heart started beating. I didn't know what to do or say. I wanted to jump up, grab his arm, and pull him out of the classroom to explain. I needed to explain to him that I hadn't been lying—not on purpose. I wanted to tell him that this was all a mistake. But I knew I couldn't and so I just sat there.

"Class, I want to introduce you to multi-billionaire Brandon Hastings. Mr. Hastings, meet the freshmen business students of Columbia University." Brandon smiled at the crowd and nodded, but his eyes sought mine. They looked shocked and angry, and I felt deeply ashamed of myself. I wanted to scream at Professor Wright for telling him we were all freshmen. I wasn't even going to be able to pretend that I was a senior. I felt immediately angry at myself for even thinking of replacing one lie with another.

The talk seemed to pass by like a flash of lightning. I was surprised because I had thought it would drag on. But somehow hearing Brandon's voice soothed me. He sounded normal, happy even, and I was able to convince myself that everything was going to be okay. But then the class ended and he walked out with the professor without even giving me a second glance.

I sat at the back of the room for about five minutes, unsure of what to say and do. I felt frozen to my seat. I was scared to leave the room and face what was to come. I didn't want to go to my study group and I didn't want to go home. I felt a tear sliding down my face as I sat there. I wanted my mom. I wanted to go home and hide in my bed and forget everything. I wanted to pretend like none of this had happened. I wanted to pretend I hadn't seen the look of anger and distrust in Brandon's eyes. I wanted to pretend that my heart didn't feel like it was cracking.

I stood up slowly and walked to the door with my heart in my mouth. I felt like my world was about to end and I didn't know how to stop it.

"Hey." Brandon was standing outside the door as I walked out.

"Hey." I smiled at him, happy to see him. For a moment I thought that everything was okay. I reached over to kiss him and he pulled away in disgust.

"No." He shook his head. "We need to talk."

"I'm sorry, Brandon." I rushed out. "I wanted to tell you, but I didn't know how."

"How old are you?" He looked at me and studied my face and body as if seeing me for the first time.

"Eighteen," I mumbled.

"What?"

"I'm eighteen."

"Not twenty-two?"

"No, I'm not twenty-two."

"Jesus Christ!" he exclaimed and then swore.

"It doesn't change how I feel about you." I reached out to touch his face and he recoiled away from me.

"It changes everything, Katie." His voice was loud. "You're a fucking freshman in college."

"I still love you."

"You don't even know what love is." He spat out the words and looked at me in disgust. "I can't believe you lied to me! You've been lying to me all this time. How could you?"

"I didn't mean to lie." I felt my eyelids getting heavy. "It's not something I intended to do."

"What was the text message all about?" He pulled out his phone. "I was going to buy you fucking flowers, Katie. I was going to buy you flowers and take you to dinner to congratulate you."

"I'm sorry." I looked down ashamed.

"So where did the promotion come from? Is it because I told you I wanted to have kids with you? Did you need to figure out a reason to get out of committing to me?"

"No, that's not it!" I cried out. "That's not why. I have to go home for Christmas," I said slowly. "My parents expect me to come home over Christmas break."

"Oh my god, your parents." His eyes looked glazed. "That's why you've never told them about me and why I've never met your friends. They don't know about me, do they?"

"They do! At least my friends do." I bit my lower lip. "I was scared for you to meet them. They all look their age."

"You mean you were worried that I would wonder why all my girlfriend's friends were eighteen and in college?" He laughed bitterly. "Or were you going to ask them to lie to me as well?"

"No, of course not." I reached for his hand. "Please, Brandon. Don't be like this. I love you."

"You love me?" He laughed a deep sorrowful sound. "You love me, huh?"

"Yes," I nodded bleakly. "I really do love you."

"Then prove it to me."

"How?"

"Fuck me."

"Huh?" I looked at him confused.

"Let's go outside and find somewhere to fuck."

"What do you mean?"

"If you love me, you will do anything I want to make me happy, right?"

"Yes, of course." I swallowed and followed him out of the building.

"Follow me." He grabbed my arm and dragged me besides him. We walked to the front of the library and then to the side of the building by the trash bins. "Pull your skirt up and bend over."

"What?" I frowned as he pushed me forward and lifted my skirt up before pulling my panties down.

"I want to fuck you."

"Here?" I looked at him like he was crazy. Anyone could walk around the corner and see us.

"Yes, here." He unzipped his pants and pulled his cock out before rubbing the tip against my opening. "Shit, you're wet already," he groaned as he slowly entered me.

"Oh, Brandon." I groaned as he filled me up.

"I love you, you know that, right, Katie?" he grunted as he pushed me toward the garbage cans. "Hold on tight. This is going to be hard and fast."

"I love you too, Brandon," I moaned, not caring in that moment if anyone heard or saw me. "Please forgive me."

"Shh." He moved faster and faster, and I gripped the garbage cans tight as he pummeled into me, letting all of his emotions out. He came hard and fast and his sperm ran down my leg as he pulled out mid-orgasm. "Oh, sorry." He looked down at the line of semen cascading down my leg.

"It's okay." I nodded and quickly pulled my panties up and my skirt down. "Can we talk?"

"I don't think so." He zipped his pants up. "I've got to get back to the office."

"Oh." I bit my lip. "We can do lunch if you want, like you said earlier."

"No." He shook his head. "I don't think so."

"Oh, maybe I can cook you dinner tonight?"

"No." He shook his head and looked at me with a blank stare. "I won't be there tonight."

"Oh?"

"I'll give you time to pack up your stuff."

"Pack up my stuff?" I frowned. "What do you mean?"

"I want you out by this weekend." He shrugged. "I'm sure it won't take long to pack up. You didn't bring much. I know why now."

"I don't want to move out." I bit my lower lip to stop myself from crying. "I love you."

"It's over, Katie."

"But I love you and you love me," I protested, trying to grab his arm and make him look at me.

"I don't date high school girls."

"I'm not in high school."

"Close enough. What difference do a couple of months

really make?" He looked up at me then and stared into my eyes. "Thanks for the last fuck though. It's a better memory for me to keep than in the classroom." And then he turned around and walked away. I stood there for about thirty minutes, stunned and dazed at what had happened. Tears streamed down my face and I sat on the ground, crying as my heart broke.

CHAPTER 4

"I still have some of your things," Brandon continued as we walked into the large conference room.

"Oh, you could have thrown them out." I gave him a weak smile. "I'm sure none of those clothes fit me anymore."

"Yeah, perhaps not." He shrugged and looked at my figure. I felt slightly self-conscious as he looked me over. I had definitely filled out since I was eighteen. Bigger breasts, curvier figure, bigger ass. "But I didn't know if there was anything you would have wanted to keep."

"Oh, well, thanks." I glanced at his face again, unable to stop myself from studying his features. I wanted to reach over and trace the lines of his face. It felt surreal to be standing here with him. This was the first time I'd seen him since we had broken up. I'd never gone back to the apartment after he had broken up with me. I'd gone to my dorm room and cried and cried, and Meg had comforted me when she came back after her classes. I'd felt humiliated and used. Abandoned and abused, and I hated him and myself. If only I hadn't lied. Things would have been different then. That's all I could tell myself.

Every day seemed the same and I waited by the phone anxiously, willing it to ring and for it to be him, begging me to forgive him and take him back. Only he never called. And I never called him. I was too scared that he wouldn't pick up or that he would tell me that he hated me.

I held out hope for two months and then I saw a photograph of him in the *New York Post* at some function with some blonde. They were kissing, and the caption said something like *Eligible bachelor Brandon Hastings off the market*. My heart broke and I lost all hope of reconciliation. He was done with me. Forever. And there was nothing I could do.

"It is good seeing you again." He nodded. "Welcome to Marathon Corp."

"Thank you. You too." I nodded politely, as if he weren't the guy who bent me over a garbage can, fucked me, and then dumped me.

"Try to keep telling the truth." His eyes flashed at me and he walked away.

I found a seat at the table and made sure to sit away from where he was standing. I didn't want to be anywhere near him. I wanted to avoid him as much as possible. I didn't want to hear his voice or look into his eyes. I wanted to pretend that this moment wasn't happening. If I could just pretend it wasn't happening, then maybe I could ignore the stirrings of emotion in my stomach.

I sat down and eagerly leafed through the folder, pretending that it was the most interesting thing I had seen in years. I didn't make small talk with anyone and I didn't look up. Finally, a lady announced that we were all to sit down. I stayed where I was. I felt safe here. And then *he* sat next to me.

"Seat vacant?" His voice was low as he sat down next to me, and I nodded as I screamed inside. "I hope you don't mind sitting next to the big boss."

"Not at all." I faked a smile and looked away.

"Liar," he whispered, and I looked up at him in surprise. His eyes sparkled as he stared at me. "It's driving you crazy that I'm sitting here."

"No, it's not," I stuttered, and he reached his hand under the table and touched my knee."

"I can feel your legs shaking." He leaned towards me and whispered in my ear. "I'm sure if I slipped my fingers under your skirt, your panties would be wet as well."

My eyes grew wide at his words. "What?" I gasped and pushed his hand away. "What are you doing?"

"What do you think?" He cocked his head and smiled before standing up. "Welcome to the Marathon Corp management orientation, everyone. I'm your new CEO, Brandon Hastings." He looked around the room and smiled widely. "I'm happy to meet everyone this weekend and tell you the direction I see our company going in. We're going to start off with some introductions and icebreakers, thanks to Human Resources, and then we'll take a fifteen-minute break." Everyone clapped at his words and he laughed. "I don't want you all to fall in love with me too quickly. I'm a hard man to please, and as your boss, I'll be looking for your best work. I don't take excuses or lies well, so if you want to continue working here, you will all put in your best effort." Everyone was nodding in agreement at his words, and I had a worried feeling in my stomach. Was he setting everything up like this so he could fire me?

"So why don't I start first, and then the lovely lady to my left will continue." He smiled down at me graciously and I pretended to smile back at him. "My name is Brandon Hastings, and I'm in my early forties. This is the third company I've run and it likely won't be the last. I enjoy gourmet cooking—I know, I know, it's not believable, right?" He laughed. "But I took a class with an old girlfriend and I haven't been able to shake the habit—or her." He laughed again and I could feel myself blushing. "Let's see… I currently live by myself in New York City, though that may be changing soon." He gave me a look and I stared at him, wondering what his last sentence meant. "You're next."

"Okay, thanks." I stood up and took a deep breath. "Hello everyone. My name is Katie, Katie Raymond. I'm twenty-five and a graduate of Columbia and NYU. I live in New York as well, but I'm from Florida. As chance would have it, I also took a cooking class with an ex-boyfriend, but I rarely find time to cook. I guess he got all the skills." I made a face and everyone laughed except Brandon. "Let's see," I said, warming up. "I've only worked at Marathon Corp for about a month but I love it so far, so I hope that never changes. Oh, I'm in love with French movies, even though I don't speak French."

"Maybe that's something someone taught you to love?" Brandon spoke lightly, and I smiled as I nodded at him.

"Yes, someone I loved introduced me to French movies." I stared at him as I spoke and sat down. I continued to stare at him even when the man next to me started talking. Brandon's eyes searched mine for a moment before he sighed and turned away. I felt the resolve building up in my body. I wasn't going to let him make me feel bad for what had happened. I had been young; I'd made a mistake. He couldn't hold it against me forever.

The introductions seemed to take forever, and I sat back in my chair with a fake smile on my face as I pretended to listen to what everyone was saying. I tried not to notice as Brandon's chair moved closer to mine, but there was no way to ignore the feel of his fingers as they ran up and down my leg.

"I've missed you," he leaned over and whispered in my ear. I pretended to ignore his touch and his voice and kept my face straight ahead. He pulled away from me, but his fingers continued to draw lines on my leg. I tried to shift away from him, but my movement gave him more access than I would have liked, and his fingers were able to work their way up my thigh, higher than I would have liked.

"Stop it," I finally turned my head and whispered at him.

"Stop what?" He gave me a questioning smile as his finger ran all the way up my thigh and then lightly across my panties.

"You know what," I gasped and clenched my legs. That was a mistake, because now I had trapped his hand right there. He immediately took it to his advantage and rubbed in between my legs softly. I could feel my panties growing wet before I reached down and pulled his hand out.

"That's not appropriate," I hissed at him, and he smiled.

"You didn't seem to mind before."

"That was seven years ago."

"Been counting, have we?" He raised an eyebrow and then grabbed my hand and placed it on his crotch. "You still make me hard." He left my hand there and I squeezed his cock without even thinking. It felt thick and hard, and I shifted in my seat as I thought about how much pleasure it had given me. "If you want, I'll let you go under the table and suck it." He smiled sweetly at me and I withdrew my hand quickly.

"You're an asshole," I mouthed at him.

"You made me that way," I thought he hissed back, but I wasn't sure if I had heard him correctly.

I could have dropped on my knees and thanked God when it was break time. If I had to sit there for one more minute, I might have done something I was going to regret. My head was spinning, my heart was pounding, and worst of all, I was horny as hell. I hated myself for feeling turned on by what he had done and for having daydreams of giving him a blowjob under the table as I sat there.

"Get it together," I hissed at myself as I jumped up, ran out of the room, and went to the ladies' room. I washed my face, reapplied my makeup, and just stared at my reflection. "You can do this, Katie," I repeated over and over to myself. "You only have to get through two days with him. That's it. Two days." I sighed and took a deep breath as I exited the bathroom. I groaned out loud as I saw Brandon standing there.

"Get lost, did you?"

"No."

"I'm glad you didn't fall in."

"So am I." I tried to walk past him and he grabbed my arms.

"You never called."

"What?" I blinked at him.

"You never called me after that day. You never came to pick up your stuff and you never called."

"I was waiting for you to call," I said softly and stared at him. "You never called me either."

"I'm going to be working in the office with you." He'd changed the subject abruptly and I nodded.

"Okay."

"I hope it's not going to be difficult." He ran his hands through his hair. "It's not a big office. We'll likely see each other a lot."

"I'm fine. It'll be fine," I lied as my body screamed at me.

"Good." He stepped toward me and lightly pressed his body against mine. I stared up into his eyes without backing down. I wasn't going to let him intimidate me. He took another step forward, and involuntarily I stepped back and hit the wall. He pushed up against me and I could feel his hardness against me as his breath tickled my ear.

"You feel warm."

"So do you." I stared into his eyes, not daring to breathe.

"I want to touch you." His fingers ran up my shirt. "I want to taste you again."

My body trembled under his touch, but I didn't move or say a word.

"I told you once that I would possess your body," he whispered in my ear. "I told you that I owned you. Do you remember that?"

"Yes," I squeaked out.

"Well, I want to take what's mine." His fingers squeezed my left breast as his mouth descended on mine roughly. His tongue slipped into my mouth and my back arched into him as I tasted his sweetness once again. My hands ran up his back to his hair and I caressed his silky tresses as we kissed. We both paused as we heard footsteps, and he quickly pulled me into the women's bathroom.

"Shh." He placed a finger across my lips as his eyes sparkled. He grabbed my hands, pulled me into a bathroom stall with him, and locked the door. I didn't even have time to think. He pulled my skirt up and my panties down before his fingers caressed my already wet opening. His other hand unzipped his pants and pulled his cock out, and before I could say a word, he lifted me up and pushed me against the door. "Wrap your legs around me," he growled into my ear, and I did as he said without a word.

He plunged into me and I cried out. His hand came down on my mouth and he stopped his movements.

"You have to be quiet," he whispered and I nodded. He then leaned down and kissed me again as he fucked me harder. This was not 'I missed you, let me make love to you' sex. This was 'I've worked myself up and I need to come as fast as I can' sex.

His cock plunged into me harder and harder, and I closed my eyes and squeezed his shoulders as I once again experienced the pleasure that had ruined me for other men. I thought about Matt briefly, and a feeling of guilt swept through me. I hadn't even slept with him yet, but here I was, giving myself to Brandon. A man I hadn't seen in seven years.

"Oh yes," Brandon grunted as his body started shuddering. "Oh, yes." His movements went faster and faster and then I felt him pause. "Open your eyes, Katie."

I opened them slowly and he smiled at me, a genuine

smile I hadn't seen in years.

"I want you to come first," he whispered. "I want to feel your pussy lips trembling and gushing on me when I come." He started his movements up once again, this time moving slowly. I groaned as I felt him fill me up. "I want you to come for me, Katie." He pushed against me hard. "Are you about to come?"

"Yes," I moaned as I reached the brink of an orgasm. "I'm about to come, Brandon." And then he started moving faster again and I climaxed fast and furious, my body trembling against him as he came inside of me.

"Oh, Katie." He kissed my cheek and let me down onto the ground. "I've missed you."

I straightened my skirt and looked up at him with a shy smile. "I've missed you too, Brandon." Our eyes connected for a few brief seconds before he opened the door. "I'll go out first." He ran his hands over his shirt and zipped up his pants. "You should wait a couple of minutes. We don't want to give anyone any ideas."

"Sure." I nodded uncertainly.

"I'm glad you took this job." He smiled at me and winked. "I think we're going to have a lot of fun."

"Thanks." I blushed, unsure of what to say, but a feeling of hope crept up in me. Maybe me getting this job and him becoming the CEO wasn't the worst thing in the world. Maybe—just maybe—this would work out for the best.

I waited for five minutes and then exited the bathroom. The hallways were empty, and I walked back into the conference room with a small smile on my face and a new pep in my step. I was disappointed when I sat down and Brandon wasn't there, but sat back and fluffed my hair, waiting for him to come back.

"Excuse me, everyone," the bitchy redhead from the table downstairs said as she walked back into the room. "You guys have an extended break for five more minutes. Mr. Hastings received an urgent call from his fiancée that he had to take. He'll be back soon." And then she casually walked out of the room as if her news hadn't just broken my heart again.

BOOK 2
CHAPTER 1

My hands gripped the table as Priscilla left the room. I stared at her retreating back with hate. I'd known she was going to be a bitch as soon as I had seen her, and now, I knew I had been right.

Her words kept spinning in my head—fiancée, fiancée, fiancée. Brandon had a fiancée? I wanted to slap myself for being so stupid, so young and naïve still. I couldn't believe I had actually believed he had been referencing me when he'd talked about not living alone for much longer. I wanted to laugh and to cry at the same time. Idiot! I was an idiot. And all I wanted to do was run out of the building and never come back.

I knew as soon as he reentered the room, because the hairs on the back of my neck stood to attention and my body froze as if sensing some impending attack. He slid into the seat next to me and I felt his hand on my shoulder.

"Don't touch me." I glared at him.

"That's a first." He raised an eyebrow at me, mocking me with his gaze.

"You have a fiancée." I tried to sound calm and not as if I was about to lose it.

"And that's a fact?"

"According to Priscilla, it is." I studied his face, hoping to God that she had been wrong.

"What did I tell you about listening to other people?" He sat back and gazed into my eyes, and I couldn't stop myself from searching for the answers in the bottomless blue ocean that was his soul. "Remember, Katie. What did I tell you the last time someone told you something about me?" His tone was soothing, and for a moment, it as if he were my Brandon again, the man I loved, and more importantly the man who loved me. As I stared into his eyes, I remembered the day he had told me to not listen to other people.

"What's wrong, poppet?" Brandon stared at me curled up on the couch, crying, and walked over to me quickly.

"Nothing," I gulped, blowing my nose on my sleeve. I looked up through wet eyelashes and tried to smile. "Are those for me?"

"Yes," he nodded as he frowned. "A guy was selling roses on the street so I got you some. I'm sorry I'm home a bit late tonight. Work has been crazy."

"It's okay." I turned my face away from his as tears threatened to fall again.

"Katie, my love. What's wrong?" He sat on the couch and pulled my face towards him. "And don't tell me nothing, I can see from your tears that you've been crying."

"Are you cheating on me?" I whispered, barely able to get the words out.

"What?" He had an incredulous look on his face and I stared into his eyes to see if he looked guilty.

"Are you seeing another woman?" I bit my lower lip and played with the bottom of my shirt.

"What are you talking about, Katie?" He shook his head. "Where is this coming from?"

"I got a phone call." I was sobbing now, unable to hold

it in. "Some lady told me that you were going to be late home tonight because you were going to be fucking her."

"What?" He looked at me in confusion, and I wondered if he had ever taken acting classes. "When did this happen? And do you have her number?"

"You don't have caller ID on the home phone," I sobbed. "And star 69 didn't work."

"Oh, she called the landline?" He sighed. "Not your cell?"

"Yes," I nodded as he pulled out a handkerchief and wiped the tears away from my eyes.

"Oh, Katie." He pulled my chin up to look at him. "I'm not cheating on you. I would never cheat on you. I love you."

"So who was that woman?" I still looked at him accusingly, though my tears were starting to dry up.

"Most probably one of my exes." He sighed and shook his head in thought. "You know I haven't been a monk. I've dated a lot of women in my life. And many of them wanted more than sex."

"So why didn't you give it to them?" I retorted, jealousy tearing through my soul as I thought about him with other women.

"Because none of them meant anything to me." His eyes pierced into mine and he just stared at me for what seemed like hours. Finally he spoke again. "You have to know that none of them meant anything to me."

"But you were engaged once." I bit my lower lip, unable to stop myself from bringing up that last point. I wanted to be his everything. The only one he'd ever loved, but he'd been engaged before and I couldn't ignore that. "You must have loved her if you wanted to marry her."

"I was young." He sighed and caressed my cheek. "I was nineteen and thought the world began and ended with Maria." I blanched at his words and he grabbed my hands. "But it didn't. I was wrong. When we're young we think that love is this big grand emotion that will consume us for the rest of our lives. That's what young love is. That's first love. That's why it feels so good and hurts so bad."

"Do you miss her?"

"No." He shook his head and laughed. "Do you miss your first love?"

"No." I whispered slowly and closed my eyes. How could I tell him that he was my first love?

"Then you know what I mean, Katie. When we were eighteen and starting college, we thought the world was at our feet and the person we dated would be the one forever. We don't even know who we are then. When I dated Maria, I thought I wanted to be an artist." He laughed. "And you know I can't draw or paint for shit."

"You're not that bad," I lied.

"I'm worse than bad," he chuckled and leaned forward to kiss me. "I proposed to Maria because I thought that was what I was supposed to do to keep her by my side when she expressed an interest in a study abroad program."

"Oh."

"It worked." He kissed my cheek. "But boy, was it a mistake. I regretted it the moment the new semester started and she was nagging me to do this and that."

"But you wanted to be with her."

"My heart and the dream in my head thought I wanted to be with her. I wanted to get a relationship right. My dad, well, he's never been a stable one-woman man. I wanted to be different from him."

"Oh, I see."

"But I proposed to Maria for all the wrong reasons. We ended up breaking up four weeks into the semester."

"What?" I looked at him in shock and he laughed.

"And she keyed my car." His hand crept up my shirt and he gasped as he touched my naked breast. "You're not wearing a bra?"

"I didn't feel like it."

"You didn't go out like this, did you?" He pulled away from me, and this time it was he who had the jealous expression.

"What if I did?"

"I don't want other men seeing you."

"I had on a top, Brandon." I rolled my eyes. "I wasn't naked."

"But still." His eyes glazed over as he looked at my chest. "Men know."

"You're just trying to change the subject," I pouted at him and pulled away.

"Katie, listen to me good. I love you. I'm with you. Yes, I was engaged once. But only because I was young and dumb. I'm not a liar and I'm not a cheat." He paused and pulled me toward him. "I won't lie to you, Katie. Know that if there is someone else, I will tell you. Don't listen to anything you hear about me unless it comes from me."

"I just want to be your number one." I melted against him as he kissed me. I felt so loved when I was with Brandon, but I also felt so insecure. I always felt like one day I was going to wake up and he was going to be done with me.

"You're my only one, Katie," he whispered against my mouth. "The only one." He pushed me back down on the couch and pulled my T-shirt up. He kissed my stomach lightly and I waited in sweet anticipation to see if his mouth was going to go north or south. My whole body was tingling in excitement as I waited to see what he was going to do.

"Do you trust me, Katie?" He raised his head and I moaned aloud, disappointed that his tongue hadn't traveled to either part of my body.

"Yes," I groaned. "Of course."

"Let's go out."

"What?" I shook my head frustrated. "I don't want to go out."

"What would you rather do?" He smiled wickedly.

"I want to make love." I groaned and reached for him. "Make love to me."

"I will." He grinned. "Eventually."

"What do you mean eventually?" I made a face.

"Let's have some fun first."

"What kind of fun?"

"I want to take you somewhere."

"Where?"

"I can't tell you."

"Why not?"

"Because then it wouldn't be a surprise."

"You never said it was going to be a surprise."

"Well, I'm saying that now." He jumped up and pulled me up with him. "Come on, Katie."

"I don't want to go." I shook my head childishly and wiped my tears away. "Not unless you tell me where we're going."

"I want to take you to an art exhibit at the Met." He sighed and shook his head. "I wanted it to be a surprise because I wanted you to meet the artist."

"Oh." I made a face. "Sorry, I didn't realize."

"And I wanted to have sex with you behind one of the sculptures." He grinned at me with vulture eyes.

"Brandon," I laughed and jumped up eagerly. "Let's go."

"You're my eager beaver." He swung me around. "If I'd known you'd be this excited, I would have told you right away."

"I like trying new things with you." I paused and touched his face. "Unless we get caught. If we get caught, I'll kill you."

"Don't worry. If you get caught and you get a record and your job finds out and they fire you, you can just come and work for me."

"Yeah, sure." I pressed my face into his chest so that he couldn't see the rising red in my face. Every time he brought up my job, I felt a burning wave of shame and horror fill me up.

"We won't get caught though." He hugged me to him. "Go and put on a dress. Not too long."

"Okay." I grinned back at him wickedly, excited about what he had planned for us.

"Oh, and Katie?"

"Yes?" I turned back to look at him as I walked into the bedroom.

"No need to put any underwear on."

"Okay." I smiled at him and he winked back at me. My body rose in temperature and I giggled as I looked through all my new dresses, deciding what to wear, all thoughts of the phone call long gone.

"You look gorgeous." Brandon's eyes widened as I walked out of the bedroom in my flowy white dress and light pink lipstick. "Your hair." He touched it lightly. "It's so wavy."

"As opposed to frizzy?" I smiled, joyous at the appreciative looks he kept giving me.

"I don't even know if I'm going to be able to leave the house." He shook his head as he kept staring at me. "Your breasts are telling me you feel the same."

"Huh?" I looked down and saw my nipples poking through my top. "Oh, maybe I should put a bra on."

"No." He shook his head. "I want easy access."

"But other guys—"

"Other guys can fuck off. You're all mine. If I even see one looking at you, they won't know what's hit them."

"Oh, Brandon." I rolled my eyes and rubbed his jaw line. "You look sexy when you don't shave."

"You like the stubble, huh?"

"Yeah." I nodded and blushed. "It tickles."

"Tickles?" He frowned, and then he grinned at me as he understood. "I guess it's a good contrast to my tongue."

"Yeah, the rough and the smooth turns me on."

"Katie," he groaned. "You don't want us to go out, do

you?" He pulled me toward him and kissed me hard, pushing his tongue into my mouth and sucking mine as if it were his favorite lollipop. I reached down and rubbed his cock. It was already hard.

"I think you're the one that doesn't want to go out anymore." I teased him as I pulled back from him. I reached my hand down his pants and held him for a few seconds before slowly running my fingers down to his balls and squeezing.

"Shit, Katie." He groaned and closed his eyes.

"Shhh," I whispered, using my hand to unzip his pants and pull his now extremely hard cock out of his pants. "No one's going to miss us if we're a few minutes late." His cock sprang free and I allowed my fingers to trace a light line along his shaft before squeezing the tip. I could feel Brandon's body tense up as he waited to see what I was going to do next. I smiled to myself as I dropped my fingers and walked away.

"Where are you going?" He slowly opened his eyes and looked at me in confused desire.

"I figured we should get going." I gave him a wicked smile and his face changed to one of surprise.

"You tease," he growled and chased me as I ran through the apartment. He caught up with me quickly and picked me up into his arms before running to the bedroom. He dropped me onto the mattress and I squealed as he lifted up my dress and buried his face in my wetness.

"I knew you were ready for me." His voice carried up to me as his tongue licked me. He gently sucked on my clit and I squirmed beneath him, wanting to feel his tongue inside of me. He continued his light licking with the tip of his tongue and allowed his stubble to graze gently against me.

"Oh, Brandon," I cried out as his tongue slowly entered me. I trembled beneath him and wrapped my legs around his neck so I could feel all of his face against my pussy. My fingers gripped his shoulder as my body built up to an orgasm. I closed my eyes in sweet anticipation as I felt myself about to explode and then he pulled away from me. "What? What are you doing?" My eyes flew open in disappointment. "Oh, Brandon. You can't stop!"

"Who's the tease now?" His eyes laughed down at me and he pulled me up off of the bed. "Now let's go."

"I hate you." I hit him in the shoulder.

"No, you don't." He laughed and grabbed my hand. "Let's go, Katie McHorny."

"Okay, Brandon McHard."

We left the apartment with glittering eyes and bodies filled with lust. My body groaned at me in frustration. It wanted a release so bad and it was all I could do to stop myself from dragging him down an alleyway and begging him to fuck me.

"Let's catch a cab." Brandon pulled me to the curb and stuck his hand out. We were lucky—a yellow cab pulled over immediately and we scrambled into the back seat. "The Met, please," Brandon told the driver, who nodded and drove off. Brandon sat back in the seat and looked out the window as I started to squirm. I couldn't stand that he looked so cool, calm, and collected while my body was begging for a release. I closed my eyes to try and stop my body from crying out.

"What's wrong?" Brandon whispered in my ear with a smirk in his voice. I turned to stare at him and give him a small glare, and I could see his eyes laughing at me.

"Nothing I can't fix." I shifted away from him and gave him a small smile.

"What do you mean?" His gaze questioned me and he gasped as he watched me pull my dress up. "You wouldn't." His eyes and his voice sounded shocked, and I just grinned at him as I closed my eyes and reached my hand in between my legs. My body shuddered as my fingers found my sweet spot, and I felt Brandon's body go still as he watched what I was doing. I leaned my head back, rested it against the headrest, and adjusted my position in the seat so I could give myself easier access. I moaned as I gently rubbed myself. I was still wet and my body was happy that it was finally going to get a release.

"What are you doing?" he hissed in my ear, and I opened my eyes slowly as I continued playing with myself.

"What does it look like?" I smiled at him, and his eyes stared into mine as my body trembled at my own touch. He moved closer to me as his hand met mine and pushed my fingers away so that it was my hand guiding his fingers up and down on my clit.

"I'm the only one who makes you come," he whispered into my ear as he increased the pace of his fingers. I didn't say anything. I was scared that if I opened my mouth I would moan or scream in ecstasy and I didn't want the cab driver to figure out what was going on. I nearly screamed when he paused and I looked at him in frustration.

"Just a second," he whispered and I saw him undoing his zipper. "Slide onto my lap."

"What?" My eyes widened. "Won't the cab driver notice?"

"It doesn't matter." He pulled me onto his lap and kissed my neck. "Oh, Katie. Stop tickling me."

I looked at him in confusion, but then I realized he was trying to vocalize a reason for being in his lap.

"You can't stop me," I giggled and almost groaned out loud as he lifted the back of my dress up and I felt his cock in between my butt cheeks.

"Move forward a little bit." He pushed me forward with his hands and lifted my hips up slightly. His hard cock slid into me easily as he sat me back down on him. "You're going to have to do the work here, Katie," he groaned in my ears as I started moving back and forth slowly. "Oh shit." His hands reached up and squeezed my breasts as I moved back and forth on his lap. His fingers squeezed my nipples and I increased my pace. I closed my eyes as we fucked in the back seat and my body shuddered as his fingers went from my breasts to my clit.

"Come for me, Katie," he whispered against my hair. "I'm going to come soon, but I need you to come for me first." The feel of his fingers rubbing against me and his cock sliding in and out of me pushed me to the edge, and my fingers dug into his thighs as I climaxed on him. I felt his arms tighten around my waist as his body shuddered and he came inside of me. He kissed my neck as we both sat back and tried to breathe. His fingers clasped mine and I leaned my head into his shoulder.

"You guys said you wanted to go to the MOMA, right?" the cab driver asked us and we laughed.

"No," Brandon finally spoke up. "You can just take us back home. Thanks though."

"I'm sorry we didn't make it to the museum." He smiled ruefully as we walked back into the apartment.

"Don't be." I tiptoed and kissed him on the lips. "I still had a good night."

"I think we both had a good night." He laughed and licked his fingers. "You know I love you, right?" He pushed me back against the wall and stared down at me. "I would never do anything to hurt you. I would never cheat on you."

"I know." I nodded breathlessly as I saw the intensity in his eyes.

"Good. As long as we are honest with each other, nothing can break us up. And I will always be honest with you, Katie. Remember, if you ever hear anything bad about me, don't believe it. Only believe it if it comes from me."

"Okay." I felt my heart bursting with love for Brandon, and I was about to tell him the truth about my age when he pulled up my dress. "What are you doing?"

"You don't think I'm done for the night, do you?" He grinned at me as his fingers found my sweet spot again. I closed my eyes as ecstasy filled me once again and all thoughts of telling him the truth fled my mind.

I shifted in my seat, feeling aroused again as I thought about that second encounter in the apartment. The sex in the cab had been hot and quick, but the sex when we got back to the apartment had been slow and sensual. So, so sensual. Brandon's fingers tapping on my knee woke me from my memories and I blinked rapidly, trying to focus on where I was.

"So you don't have a fiancée?" I looked at him hopefully with my heart in my mouth. Maybe the HR bitch had gotten it wrong. Maybe he was still the decent guy I'd known. Maybe that's why he had said our phrase. If the words hadn't come from him, it wasn't true.

"No, Priscilla was right. I do have a fiancée and I was on the phone with her." His eyes stared into mine with a challenge. I knew what he was thinking: *What are you going to do about it, Katie?* I could feel in my bones that he wanted me to react.

"But..." I shook my head in confusion. "You told me I shouldn't listen to other people. You told me that if it doesn't come from you, it's not true."

"You shouldn't listen to other people about me." He shrugged. "But I'm here now and I'm telling you that, yes, I have a fiancée."

"How could you?" I gasped, my heart breaking.

"How could I what?"

"Sleep with me," I whispered, my eyes wide.

"We didn't do any sleeping."

"How could you fuck me when you have a fiancée?" I hissed at him, mad.

He smiled then, a wide, mocking smile. His blue eyes looked down at me in disdain. "Men with power, men with money, men like me... We can do what we want, when we want, with whoever we want. I wanted to fuck you." He picked up a napkin and wiped his hands. "So I did." He turned away from me then and stood up. "Okay, everyone. Let's get back to work."

I sat there, humiliated, feeling like a slut. Once again he had made me feel cheap, like a piece of meat a dog had discarded. I listened to him talking, but I didn't hear the words that were flowing out of his mouth. As I sat there, I felt my body getting hotter and hotter. I couldn't stand it anymore. I had to leave. I didn't care if I got fired—I'd find another job. Nothing else mattered but my leaving the room, right then and there.

I jumped up as Brandon stopped talking and he grabbed my arm as I made to leave the table. "Where are you going?" His eyes were dark as his fingers pinched into my skin.

"I'm leaving." I pulled my arm away from him. "I'm not going to let you treat me like this."

"You're not going anywhere." He shook his head. "Not until I say you are."

"You can't stop me." I turned around and quickly walked out of the room. I could hear my heart beating like drums at a rock concert as I hurried out. People in the room were whispering and watching me, and I knew they were all wondering what was going on.

"Excuse Katie, everyone. She just got an important call. She'll be back in a moment." Brandon spoke up and I looked back at him with a glare. He faked a sympathetic smile and nodded at me. "Take your time, Katie. We'll be here when you get back."

"I'm not coming back," I shot back as I glared at him. I didn't care who heard me. I was done. He had no right to treat me this way. Let him explain my abrupt departure. I half-expected him to follow me out of the room, and I was disappointed when I realized he wasn't coming. I walked into the elevator and waited for him to rush out of the room and run into the elevator to stop me. Only he didn't. The doors closed slowly and the ride down seemed to take forever.

I pulled my phone out as soon as I walked out to call Meg. I needed to talk to her. I needed someone to remind me what a jerk he was so I wouldn't burst out crying.

"Hello?" Her voice was breathless, and my heart stopped beating.

"Meg, what's wrong?"

"I was fired." She burst into tears. "The law firm laid me off yesterday with no severance. They said that they couldn't afford to keep me."

"Oh, that's horrible." I leaned against the wall next to the elevator with my heart beating fast. "Can they do that?"

"Yes. I had no contract. I was an employee-at-will." Her voice broke. "I don't know what I'm going to do." She burst into tears again.

"You can just get another job, right?"

"They told me that they won't give me a reference." She sobbed hysterically. "I'm done, Katie."

"Oh, Meg." My heart broke for her, as I knew how happy she had been when she had gotten her law job.

"Thank God you have this position," she sobbed. "You don't mind covering the next few months' rent, do you? I'll pay you back as soon as I have a new job."

"Sure." My heart dropped at her words. How could I quit now? "You don't even have to ask. You know I will always be here for you."

"How is everything with you, by the way?" She sighed. "Sorry, I completely forgot to ask if you'd seen Brandon. My mind was caught up in my own issues."

"It's fine," I lied. "I saw him, but for, like, a minute. I don't even think he recognized me."

"That's good, right?" I could hear her blowing her nose. "Hopefully you won't see him again. Then you can just come back home and forget about him again."

"Yeah." My voice was weak as I spoke into the phone. "Everything is going according to plan," I lied again. Nothing was going according to plan. Nothing at all.

I closed my eyes for a moment as I thought about everything I had been through, everything I had put into action, and my heart broke again. I'd made a big mistake, and once again I was getting burned.

"So I'll see you tomorrow night, right?" Meg's voice sounded a bit happier. "I'll cook pasta and you can help me look for jobs."

"Sounds like a plan." I cleared my throat. "But I better go now. I think we're starting up again."

"Okay, great. Thanks for cheering me up. I miss you already."

"You need to get a boyfriend." I laughed, shaking my head at her words. "You won't have time to miss me then."

"I'm working on it." She giggled. "Bye, Katie."

"Bye, Meg." I put the phone back into my pocket and pressed the elevator button again. I walked into the elevator feeling defeated, deflated, and devalued. I couldn't believe that I had to go back to that room and sit next to him. I never wanted to see him again. He had made me feel like a cheap slut once again and I hated him for it. I hated the man he now was. How could he have a fiancée and sleep with me?

The elevator stopped and I walked out, deep in thought. I had only taken two steps when I heard his voice against my ear as he pushed me up against the wall.

"What are you doing?" I struggled against him, trying to stop my racing heart from being so excited at being close to him again.

"I told you. You don't leave until I say." His eyes were dark as he looked down at me. His fingers traced the lines of my trembling lips. "Don't ever walk out on me again."

"Or what?" I squared my shoulders and looked back at him with fire in my eyes. This wasn't over. Not by a long shot.

CHAPTER 2

"So I'm looking for us to make a profit by quarter three." Brandon's voice was passionate as he talked about his plans for the company. "That means we're all going to have a lot of late nights." He looked around the room, and his eyes fell on me for a brief second before moving on. "Does anyone have any questions?"

"Will we be getting raises anytime soon?" a guy across the table asked seriously and some others nodded.

"Let's talk about raises when we actually start seeing a profit." Brandon's tone was brusque. "Anything else?"

"Excuse me, Mr. Hastings." Priscilla walked into the room and interrupted the meeting.

"Yes?" he snapped.

"Maria is on the phone again and she says it's an emergency."

"Okay." He nodded and jumped up. "Excuse me, everyone. I'll be right back." He walked out of the room, and I sat there in stunned immobility. Had Priscilla just said Maria? It couldn't be the same Maria, could it? Not the one he had been engaged to when he was in college? My heart started racing, and I felt like I couldn't breathe. All my insecurities came flooding back and I wanted to scream and shout. Had he lied to me before? Had he really always been in love with her? I wanted to cry and bury my face in a pillow. Maybe everything I had thought we had was false. What if I had just been someone to pass the time while he tried to forget about his true love, Maria?

I stood up quickly and walked out of the room. I needed to get some fresh air or I was going to cry. I knew it by the pain in my head and the tightness in my eyes. I rushed down the corridor and to the elevator. I breathed a sigh of relief as the elevator arrived and I ran out when I arrived on the ground floor. I hurried to the outside and was grateful that I didn't see Brandon as I made my way out. I took two deep gulps of air and pulled out some gum to chew to calm my nerves.

"Cat got your tongue?" His voice was smooth and melodic, and I jumped slightly.

"Sorry, I didn't see you there."

"I didn't know I said anyone could leave the room."

"I didn't know that we had to wait for permission." I shrugged.

"I thought you were going to quit." He changed the subject.

"I had a change of mind." I looked at the ground to avoid staring into his eyes. They still made my heart leap and sing, and my stomach was doing flip-flops as he stared at me.

"It's funny how that happens." He smiled at me and took a step towards me. "You look just the same, you know." He studied my face and then my body. "More of a woman, but just the same."

"I'm not sure if that's a compliment." I smiled and then looked him over. "You look the same as well."

"Now that's a lie." He laughed. "I'm greying now." He pointed to his hair and I noticed a few grey streaks. However, to me, they only made him look more distinguished and sexy.

"It doesn't detract from your good looks." I made a face at him and we both laughed.

"You always were the most honest person I knew," he

said wistfully, and an awkward silence befell us at the irony of his words.

"I guess we should go back up." I put my gum away and started walking toward the main entrance.

"Wait." He grabbed ahold of my arm and stopped me.

"What?" I looked at his hand with a frown.

"There was a time when you didn't regard my touch as something bad."

"There was a time when you didn't have a fiancée when you slept with me."

"There was a time when I wanted you to be my fiancée."

"What do you want, Brandon?" I sighed and pulled away from him.

"I want us to forget our past. Let's move on."

"Maybe you should have thought of that earlier in the day."

"I can still feel your body shaking as I fucked you in the bathroom." He groaned. "It felt as good as I remembered."

"Stop it." I shook my head.

"Did it feel as good for you?" He wrapped his hands around my waist and pulled me toward him. "Did my cock give you as much pleasure as it used to?"

I remained silent as he whispered in my ear, his hands grabbing my ass. He stared into my eyes searchingly and I just stared back, unblinking.

"You're shivering." His lips neared mine. "You're shivering, but it's not cold outside." His lips lightly pressed against mine. "You're shivering because you want me to fuck you again."

"Get your hands and your lips off of me." I pushed him away. "What would Maria say if she could see you?"

"That's none of your business." His eyes darkened.

"You're making it my business."

"Are you single, Katie?" He cocked his head and his eyes studied my fingers as I nervously played with my hair.

"From your reaction, it seems to me as if you're also seeing someone. Does that then mean that you're no better than me?"

"Matt isn't my fiancé." I shot back, though I did feel all sorts of guilty. There were many things Matt didn't know about me.

"I'm sure he would love to know that you don't feel you need to be faithful to him because he isn't your fiancé." He shook his head. "But I suppose you like to keep all sorts of things to yourself."

"Is it the same Maria?" I couldn't stop myself from asking. I had to know.

"Is what the same Maria?"

"Are you engaged to the same Maria you were engaged to when you were in college?"

"It's none of your business." He looked away then and my heart fell. In my heart I knew it was her. "What are you doing this evening?"

"Why?"

"I have a business meeting." He looked at his watch. "With some Japanese businessmen. They're bringing their wives. It would be smarter for me to go with someone."

"Take Maria."

"She's in New York."

"I see." I bit my lip. I wanted to know if he lived with her. I was annoyed at myself. There were so many stones I had left unturned. I shouldn't be this unaware of what was going on in his life.

"So, I'll pick you up at your hotel at seven p.m.?"

"I didn't say yes."

"You're staying at the Diva, right?"

"Yeah." I looked up at him in surprise. "How did you know?"

"Just had a feeling. How'd you like those purple lights?"

"Fine." I looked away again, feeling uneasy.

"I'll end the session today at four." He smiled and

86

started walking back toward the entrance. "That should give you enough time to get ready and do your hair."

"Who says I'm going to do anything with my hair?" I raised an eyebrow at him.

"I'd rather you didn't, actually. You know I prefer it wild and crazy." He paused by the main entrance and opened the door for me. "Especially when you were riding me and climaxing. It made me feel like Tarzan, with my wild Jane." He whispered in my ear as I walked past him, "I miss fucking my wild Jane."

I ignored him and continued walking to the elevator. I was not going to let him intimidate me or make me feel embarrassed. He knew how to push my buttons and was doing everything he could to get a rise out of me. I smiled to myself as a plan hatched in my mind while I walked into the elevator. I would show him who could play a smarter game. I was about to call his bluff, and I was going to enjoy doing it.

***

I walked out of the elevator and into the lobby in a long red dress. It had a plunging neckline and a high slit. I wore the dress with pride, and I knew that my accompanying stilettos made me look hot. I was going for sex appeal tonight, and if the looks of all the men in the lobby were anything to go by, I had achieved the look quite successfully.

Brandon was sitting on a chair waiting for me, and my heart stopped when our eyes met. I saw the look of surprise, desire, and lust as he took me in. Then he smiled at me—a warm, gentle smile that reminded me of when we first met—and I was taken back to the days when we were friends and lovers.

"You look beautiful, Katie." He stood up and reached for my hand. "I see you're finding it easier to walk in heels."

"Not really," I giggled, already slightly buzzed from the two glasses of red wine I had enjoyed while getting dressed. "I may need to hold your arm as we walk."

"That's fine." He held out his arm for me. "I'll be your knight in shining armor. I'll be there to catch you if you fall."

"Thank you." I smiled at him and my heart constricted as I remembered the last time he had said those words to me. We'd been in Central Park on a picnic. I'd been expecting him to pull out a blanket for us to lie down under so that we could have a quickie, but he'd surprised me by pulling out some rollerblades.

"No way." I shook my head vehemently. "I have no balance. No way I'm rollerblading."

"Come on, Katie." He pulled me up. "It'll be fun."

"I'm going to fall."

"I won't let you fall." He pulled me towards him. "I'll never let you fall."

"I'm a klutz. Trust me, I'll fall."

"I'll be your knight in shining armor. I'll be there to catch you if you fall." He kissed the top of my head, and I could hear his heart beating as I laid my head against his chest. I looked up at him, and sincerity and love were pouring out of his eyes. I leaned into him and pressed my lips on his. Our kiss was sweet and special and filled with promises. In that moment, I knew that Brandon would always be in my heart and I would always be in his. We were connected as one.

"Then come on." I laughed and pulled off my shoes. "Let's go rollerblade before I change my mind."

And we'd spent the rest of the day holding hands and rollerblading through Central Park, and I hadn't fallen once.

"Shall we go?" Brandon smiled at me gently and I nodded. We made our way out of the hotel and I nearly tripped as he stopped suddenly. "I want to apologize."

"Oh?" My heart stopped as I held on to his arm.

"What I did today, it was wrong. I shouldn't have taken advantage of you."

"You didn't take advantage of me." I made a face. "I was willing and able to say no."

"I couldn't help myself." He sighed. "When I saw you in the elevator, I couldn't believe it. I'd been waiting for—anticipating, even—that moment forever. And I just got caught up in myself."

"I guess no one can say we don't have sexual chemistry."

"I want you to know something." He held my hands and caressed them. "I want you to know that what Maria and I have... It's not what it seems."

"She's not your fiancée?" I asked him hopefully, but my heart fell as he shook his head.

"She is, but it's complicated." He made a face. "So tell me about this guy you're dating. Did you say his name was Matt?"

"Yeah." I nodded. "He's a nice guy, very dependable. Seems to like me a lot."

"Really?" He frowned. "Close to engagement?"

"I don't know."

"Does he make your body tremble when he fucks you?"

"No." I sighed as I continued. "We haven't slept together yet."

"Oh." He smiled. "I see."

"We're waiting so that we can make it special. Relationships and sex are about more than some quick fucks," I said spitefully, wanting to hurt him.

"But sometimes the quick fucks are the best ones." His hands crept up my back. "Sometimes, you want your man to just push you up against the wall." He grabbed ahold of me and pushed me back. "Sometimes, you want him to take charge and slide his hand around your waist and push himself into you, so that you can feel his hard erection against your stomach."

He pushed into me then and I felt his hardness against me. I stared up into his eyes wanting to stop him but also wanting to see how far he was going to take this. He adjusted himself so that his leg was in between mine, and his cock was positioned by my inner thigh.

"Sometimes, you dream of your man bending his head"—his lips moved to my neck and his tongue trailed to my collar bone—"and lowering his lips." He kissed down the valley in between my breasts and I stood there, frozen, not caring if anyone was walking past us and wondering what was going on. "Sometimes you want your man to show you who's the boss." His hand reached up my stomach and stopped right below my breast before slipping into the top of my dress and caressing my breast. "Because, Katie…" He looked up at me with a light in his eyes as he squeezed my nipple. "Women like to be possessed. They like to be taken. They like to feel sexy and sensual, and they want to feel loved."

He leaned forward and kissed me hard as his hand pushed the top of my dress to the side. He bent his head quickly and took my nipple in his mouth, sucking it eagerly and nibbling on it as he would candy. I closed my eyes as ripples of pleasure swept through me. My hands fell to his head and ran through his hair as he sucked. I let out a whimper as he released me from his warm embrace and then sighed again in relief as he transferred his lips to the other nipple.

I felt my knees buckling as his arm wrapped around my waist and held me against him and the wall firmly. His erection pushed into me even more urgently, and I reached my fingers down to squeeze it gently. I tried to unzip his pants, but he pushed my hand away and pulled away from me.

He looked at me and smiled. "You see, Katie? Sometimes the quick fucks are the most exciting and exhilarating. Sometimes they turn you on more than you seem to want to admit. Unfortunately, this is not your lucky night." His eyes mocked me as he moved away from me completely. "Tonight, you will have to hope that your boyfriend, Michael or Tad or whatever his name is, gets some gumption and makes a move soon. Because, little girl, tonight will not be the night that you get any from me, no matter how sexy your dress is."

I swallowed hard as I looked at him, completely dazed. I wasn't sure what had just happened. Minutes ago, he had been apologizing to me, and I thought we were finally going to put everything behind us. But yet again he had my head spinning in anger and my body aching for his touch.

I didn't say anything to Brandon as we walked to the restaurant. Instead, I just mentally confirmed my plan for the night. Brandon was right and wrong. He was right about the fact that sometimes a woman just wanted a man to take charge and take her, but he was wrong about the fact that he wasn't going to be fucking me tonight. If I had anything to do with it, I was going to have him shouting my name and begging me to forgive him for all the shit he had pulled on me. As far as I was concerned, he had gotten away with far too much. I wasn't a woman he could use and abuse like some pawn in a game of chess. He was about to find out that he wasn't the only piece of royalty on the board, and I was about to get into the game. And this time, I was playing to win.

CHAPTER 3

"Konnichiwa."

"Konnichiwa."

I stood there and smiled at the wives of the Japanese businessmen Brandon was meeting for dinner. I felt out of place in my revealing dress, as they were all dressed very conservatively. Their wives looked at me with polite smiles, but I could see the question in their eyes. *Is she a prostitute?* I was embarrassed for all of two minutes before I realized that ultimately it was Brandon who would look like the fool.

"They like you." He smiled at me as we walked to the table. He was back to being nice again, but I couldn't tell if he was being genuine or putting on a show.

"I feel like maybe I wore the wrong outfit for a business dinner." I made a face. "Sorry."

"Why are you apologizing?" He squeezed my hand. "You look sexy as hell, yes, but I'm not complaining. I like dining with a beautiful woman at my side."

"Oh." I blushed at his words. "Thank you."

"No need to thank me for telling the truth." He pulled my chair out as we reached the table and then sat next to me. "This is nice." He looked around the restaurant and smiled. "It's been a while since we've gone out to eat together."

"Yes, it has."

"This time you can even order alcohol if you want to."

"Funny." I looked away from him and he laughed.

"Don't tell me I can't make jokes about your age. Not after all the laughs you had on my behalf."

"What are you talking about?" I glared at him. "What laughs?"

"All the laughs you and your friends had when you told them what a fool I was for believing all your lies."

"I never thought you were a fool."

"I was a fool." He sighed. "I don't know how I didn't figure out you were eighteen."

"I guess I was a good actress."

"That's the problem. You weren't." He chuckled. "When I think back to everything now, it's all so clear to me. How eager and happy you were all the time to see me, how open you were with your feelings. The fact that you were a virgin and the fact that you were always willing and eager to do whatever I wanted to do sexually."

"Not everything." I shook my head.

"That's true." He licked his lips as he stared at me. "I never got you to agree to anal."

"Would you like to see the wine menu?" A waiter appeared at our side, and I looked at him with a small smile while dying of mortification inside.

"Thank you." Brandon took the menu and opened it so we could both see.

"Mr. Kai, would you like me to order the wine?" Brandon addressed the only person in the business party who appeared to speak English.

"Thank you, Mr. Hastings. We would like that very much." Mr. Kai nodded and then spoke to the others rapidly in Japanese.

"I don't think I'm going to be able to help much," I whispered to Brandon. "I don't speak much Japanese."

"Your presence alone is enough." He squeezed my knee and smiled at me. I tried not to pull away from him, but every time he touched me, I felt like I was flying and it was hard for me to come back down to earth.

"I think we're all going to have a less fatty steak tonight. I'm guessing everyone will have a filet mignon, don't you think?" Brandon spoke out loud as he studied the wine menu. "So I guess I'll choose a bottle that has a bit less tannin."

"How do you know?" I asked, interested.

"I tried to be a sommelier when I was in my twenties." He looked up at me. "And I worked at a couple of wineries in Napa and Sonoma."

"I never knew that before."

"There are a lot of things you don't know about me, Katie."

"Have you decided on your wine?" The waiter reappeared, and I sat back while I waited for Brandon to order.

"Let's see. We're definitely going to go with a cabernet sauvignon." He studied the menu and looked up at the waiter. "Will you check and see if you have a 2002 Abreu cabernet sauvignon from the Thorevilos Vineyard Napa Valley in the cellar, please?"

"Wines in the cellar start at $500, sir."

"That's fine." Brandon shrugged. "That's the wine we want, if you have it. Two bottles would be better than one."

"I'll go and check now, sir." The apathetic-looking waiter's eyes lit up as he quickly departed the table.

"That's too much money." I whispered at him. "You can't spend $500 on wine."

"If they have a bottle, it'll be about $850, actually." He smiled at me and his eyes crinkled. "I have billions, Katie. There's no need to be worried. Consider it a catch-up drink for all those nights I took you out to dinner and you only got a water."

"Yeah, but we're not dating anymore."

"Whose fault is that?" His fingers caught mine and he

squeezed them until I looked up at him. "Don't tell me what to do, Katie."

"I'm not telling you what to do."

"You made me lose control in my life once. I'm not going to let you do that to me again."

"What?" I frowned, but then Mr. Kai started talking about business, so I just sat back and smiled at the other women in the group. They smiled at me politely and I smiled back, not knowing what else to do.

The waiter hurried back to the table with a huge smile. "Sir, we've found two bottles for you. Would you like to do a tasting?"

"Yes," Brandon nodded and raised his glass, and the waiter popped the cork and poured a sampling into his glass. Brandon gave it a quick sniff, swirled it in his glass, and then sipped. He allowed the wine to sit in his mouth for a moment before he swallowed. "Delicious." He nodded at the waiter. "I like it a lot. The wine is deep, well-balanced, and complex." He turned to me. "Just like I like my women."

"So you two married, yes?" One of the women on the other side of the table leaned forward. "Happy couple?"

"Yes." Brandon nodded and I sat back with a fake smile on my face.

"She is younger than you?" Mr. Kai questioned and looked back and forth at us. I was surprised at the bluntness of his question.

"Much younger." Brandon nodded. "But what does age matter when it comes to love?"

Mr. Kai didn't respond but instead seemed to explain the conversation to the others at the table. Some of the women's eyes changed from polite to accepting and I realized, now that they thought I was the wife, everything was okay.

"What sort of business dinner is this?" I whispered in Brandon's ear. "Only one of them speaks English, and I can't imagine this is a setting where any deals are going to get made."

"The Japanese culture is different from ours, Katie." Brandon kissed my cheek as he whispered, "This may seem like an informal dinner to you, but it is also a vetting process. A process where they will evaluate whether I am someone they think they can trust."

"At a dinner?" I raised an eyebrow.

"Yes, at a dinner." He pulled away from me and raised his glass. *"Kanpai."*

"Kanpai." They raised their glasses and smiled back.

I lifted up my glass and repeated the phrase they had used. *"Kanpai."* I took a sip of the wine and immediately felt soothed. This was a good glass of wine, indeed.

"Enjoying it?" Brandon looked at me as I continued sipping and I nodded. "It's a very delicate wine. The blueberry, boysenberry jam, vanilla, licorice, chocolate, truffle, earth, and smoke scream from the glass, don't they?"

"I, uh, guess." I laughed. "I mean, I do taste some blueberry, I think."

"I'll have to teach you about wine one of these days." His eyes danced as I took another sip. "There's a vineyard in Napa, owned by some family friends, that I love. They have a castle, and I always thought it would make a romantic trip."

"It sounds like it." I smiled back at him, but I wanted to question him. Was he saying that because he really wanted to take me or because he was playing a role?

"How long you two been in love?" the one lady who seemed to know some English asked. I felt tongue-tied and nervous at her question. I was scared that it would be obvious to Brandon that I still loved him if I answered.

"I think I've loved Katie from the moment I first met her," Brandon responded. "My heart only began beating the moment I met her." He stared at me with love in his eyes, and his fingers brushed a piece of hair away from my face. "She was my angel. She found me at a time when I

97

was in an emotionally bad place. She saved me from myself. Her love, her beauty, her kindness, her love of life—they saved me."

"Oh, Brandon." My heart melted at his words, and I reached over and grabbed his hands. "I feel the same way." I couldn't stop the words from gushing out of my mouth. "I feel like I was made to love you, that a part of you has always been in me, just waiting for us to meet."

The couples across the table stared at us, not really understanding what we were saying but feeling the love flowing between us.

"I knew you were the one for me in the very beginning," Brandon continued in a soft tone, but then his eyes hardened as they looked at me. "I think a large part of it was your honesty. I always knew that, no matter what happened, we would always have the truth. And I knew that nothing could break up a couple that has the truth on its side." He pulled away from me, still smiling, and I felt a deep pain shatter my heart as he hammered the nail in.

He was never going to forgive me. It didn't matter that it had been seven years since the lie. Seven years for him to get over what I had done. He was determined to continue making me pay for what I had done. Taking this job had been a mistake. Everything had been a big mistake. I lectured myself to stop trying to give him second chances and to stop hoping for the impossible. How much more did he have to tell me or do before I would accept that we were over forever? All I had left to do was to do to him what he had done to me. I was going to fuck him and then leave him as if he meant nothing to me. I knew that it might not break his heart, but it would definitely hurt his pride, and that was all I could hope for right now.

***

"Did you enjoy dinner?" Brandon was polite and distant as we walked away from the restaurant. The dinner had gone well, and his guests had gone off in their taxis looking fairly pleased. I wasn't sure if it was due to the wine or the company though. The two bottles of wine had turned to five, and we had all been a bit jolly by the end of the meal.

"I had a good time. They were nice." I walked slowly, trying not to stumble. He placed his arm in front of me, but I ignored it.

"Let me guide you, Katie. I don't want you to fall."

"No, thanks." I shook my head. "I'm fineeeee." My words slurred slightly and I giggled.

"You're drunk."

"No, I'm not," I hiccupped.

"Katie." He sighed and pulled me toward him. "Hold on to me."

I wrapped my arms around him and pushed my breasts against him as I let my left hand fall down casually and brush against the front of his pants. His body grew tense as he held on to me and I kissed his neck.

"Let's go dancing," I whispered in his ear, letting my tongue lick his inner ear before I nibbled on his earlobe.

"You should really get home." He shook his head, but I could see desire emanating from his every pore.

"I don't wanna go home yet." I hiccupped again. "Let's go dancing. I know a place."

"How do you know a place?"

"I saw it yesterday." I grabbed his hand. "Please." We stood there in the middle of the street, and he closed his eyes and took a deep breath.

"Fine. We can go for an hour. That's it."

"That's all the time I need," I whispered to him as excitement filled me. An hour was going to be more than enough time.

"Welcome to the club." A scantily clad lady ushered us into 'The X Room' and I pretended that I didn't notice Brandon's look of surprise as we walked into the dark club.

"Katie," he hissed as I dragged him towards the booming music. "What sort of club is this?"

"I don't know," I lied. "I just want to dance."

"Katie." He grabbed my hand to try to pull me back, but I just laughed and pulled away from him. I pushed my way through the crowds of men until I found an empty booth in the side of the room and sat down. "Katie." His eyes narrowed as he sat next to me. "This is a strip club. We can't do any dancing here."

"Yes, we can." I moved into him. "I can dance for you."

"What do you mean?"

"I mean, I want to dance for you."

"Dance for me?"

"Or would you rather I said strip?"

"Katie, I don't know." He looked around and then back at me. "This isn't what I had in mind for tonight."

"Just because you didn't plan it doesn't mean it can't happen." As I spoke, I thought back to everything I knew about Brandon, and I realized that several things were starting to add up. "You like to be in control, don't you, Brandon?" I stood up and straddled him as I spoke to him.

"What man doesn't?" He shrugged.

"No, I mean, you need to be in control. Everything about you screams it." I shook my head in wonder. "I'm not sure how I never realized that before."

"I don't know what you're talking about."

"What was your life like before we met?" I pulled my dress up at the sides so that I could rub back and forth on him more easily. "I know you had lots of flings and you were focused on your job, but I didn't really know you." My eyes gazed into his as I kissed him lightly. He stared back at me with a guarded expression.

"It doesn't really matter now, does it?"

"It doesn't matter, but I want to know." I started unbuttoning his shirt and kissing down his neck to his chest. I gasped as his hand ran up my dress and grasped my ass.

"Hey, guys," A cute topless girl walked up to us. "You're welcome to do what you want, but if you want to remain in the booth, you need to order a bottle."

"A bottle of what?" I questioned.

"Champagne, Katie," Brandon laughed. "We'll have a bottle of Dom, please."

"Coming right up." The girl shook her breasts at Brandon and he smiled at her appreciatively.

"I can't believe you were staring at her breasts."

"What?" He looked at me with a bemused expression. "You can't be serious. You brought me to a strip club and now you're upset when I check out another ladies' tits."

"I'm not jealous." I bent my head and bit his shoulder. I didn't want to analyze my feelings too closely because he was right. I was pissed at the girl for flirting with him and even madder at him for seeming to enjoy the view. My inner brain was screaming at me, *She's the least of your concerns, Katie. He has a fiancée.* "It doesn't matter to me."

"Sure." He laughed and his expression seemed more relaxed. "Why don't you continue with your dance?" His hands pushed against my ass and brought me in closer to him. "Dance for me and I'll see how many singles I have."

"What?" I frowned as I realized that the mood had changed. I had gone from being in control and having the power to being his personal plaything. I knew that if I continued with my 'seducing him in the strip club' plan, I would be the one who ended up feeling hurt at the end of the night. I continued to grind back and forth on him and he reached up and pulled the top of my dress down so that my breasts were rubbing against his chest.

"Move a little bit faster," he groaned in my ear as his fingers slipped inside of my panties and rubbed me. "That's it." His voice was devious as he slipped his fingers inside of me. I continued moving, but I felt conflicted inside. I wanted him so badly, but not like this. Not with him calling the shots.

I jumped up quickly and rubbed my head. "I'm not feeling well." I made a face. "I'll be back." I hurried away to find the bathroom before I quickly washed my face with water and drank some to clear my head. I didn't know what I was going to do. My plan had been to pretend I was really drunk, take him to the strip club, fuck him, and leave. But it would only work if he wasn't the one in control. Now he was the one guiding me. He was the one turning me on. If we had sex in that booth, it was going to be him leaving me and making me feel guilty. I wasn't going to let that happen. Tears fell from my eyes as I stared in the mirror at my reflection. Who was I becoming? It was one thing for me to have this plan when I thought he was single, but now I knew he had a fiancée and I was still going through with everything. How could I do this to another woman? I took another gulp of water and walked back through the flashing lights, loud music, and naked women knowing I had made a mistake.

"Are you okay?" Brandon jumped up as soon as I reached the booth and he stared at me in concern. "What's wrong?"

"Nothing." I shook my head and avoided eye contact with him.

"What's wrong, my Katie?" He pulled me toward him, his fingers nudging my chin up to look at him.

"Nothing." I averted my gaze.

"Hey, guys. The Dom is here." The half-naked waitress came back and I wanted to groan.

"Set it on the table, thanks." Brandon's eyes never left mine. "Katie," he continued. "I know something is wrong. I can see it in your eyes. Tell me what's wrong?"

"I want to go home," I mumbled, my insides crumbling as he held me against him.

"I'm not letting you go anywhere unless you tell me what's wrong." His voice was adamant and he pulled me down to the couch to him. "Katie." His fingers caressed my cheeks. "Please tell me what's wrong."

"I'm just not feeling good."

"Do you need me to take you to the doctor?" His eyes looked worried as I shook my head. Why was he being so nice? He was making this so much harder on me. I didn't want to be reminded of how caring he was. "Need me to play doctor?" He grinned and I shook my head as he made a funny face. "'Cause I can play doctor, you know that, right?"

"Hmm, I think I remember you made a pretty good doctor once upon a time."

"I know. Once upon a time, I nursed you back to health and became the luckiest man in the world." His eyes caught mine and we just stared at each other for a moment. In that moment, I felt like the last seven years hadn't happened.

"I was very lucky that night," I whispered as he kissed my cheek.

"I was going to propose, you know."

"What?" I stared at him in shock.

"That was going to be my Christmas gift." He rolled his eyes. "Corny, I know. I was going to do it at my parents' house on Christmas Eve. I had it all planned."

"I had no idea." My heart raced as I stared at him. "You never told me."

"It wouldn't have been a Christmas surprise if I had told you."

"I'm sorry I lied." I looked down at my lap. "I guess I never really got to say it before. But I'm really sorry. I didn't mean to deceive you."

"Shh." He shook his head and grabbed my hand. "Let's go."

"But what about the Dom?"

"What about it?" He laughed and grabbed the bottle up before throwing some bills on the table. "We're taking it with us."

"Where are we going?"

"Back to my apartment."

"Oh."

"If that's okay?" he asked me softly, a question in his eyes.

"Yes." I nodded slowly. *Just one more night,* I thought to myself. I just needed one more night to get him out of my head.

***

His apartment reminded me of the one we had shared in New York. It had the same homey yet masculine feel, and I immediately felt at ease. We walked into the apartment urgently and our lips fell upon each other as soon as he closed the door. He picked me up and placed the Dom under his arm as he carried me.

"Where are we going?" I looked up at him as he walked past what appeared to be his bedroom door.

"To the guest bathroom. It has a bigger tub than in my room."

"Oh, why?"

"One of the best memories I have is of the time we made love in the shower." He grinned at me. "I've thought about it many times. I want to make some memories in the tub now."

"Oh." I blushed as he reminded me of the night we had made love in the shower. It had been during our experimentation stage and many sex toys had been involved.

"Come here." He pulled me toward him and kissed me hard. I lifted my arms up and he pulled my dress off before admiring my naked breasts. "Shit, you're sexy."

"You're not so bad yourself." I pulled his shirt off and then his pants. "You're not wearing any briefs?"

"I was hoping to have some fun tonight."

"You were?" I frowned at him. "But you said earlier that I was going to be disappointed. You said you had no plans to fuck me."

"I lied." He laughed and his eyes clouded over. "You don't have the monopoly on that, you know."

I leaned forward and kissed him hard, wanting him to shut up so he didn't ruin the moment. His fingers played with my hair and then he slowly pulled away. "Don't pout, I'm just running the bath." He turned the tap on and then poured a liquid into the tub. It started foaming up right away and I grew excited.

"Are you sure we're both going to fit?"

"Yes." He reached over, slipped my panties off, and then got into the tub. "Are you going to join me?" He smiled and reached a hand out for me and I took it gratefully. I stepped into the tub and stood there, not sure where to sit. "Sit on my lap." He pulled me down towards him and I sat with my back towards him. When he reached over and touched something, all the lights went out. We sat there in the tub in silence for a few seconds as the bubbles filled up the bath.

Brandon grabbed a washcloth and started bathing me. His hands rubbed my neck and my shoulders then fell to my breasts and my stomach. "Spread your legs. Let me clean you," he whispered in my ear, and he used the washcloth to wash my private area.

I melted back into him, enjoying the feel of his strong hands as they moved the warm, soapy washcloth along my body. I closed my eyes and rubbed his legs as he continued to clean me. I moaned as I felt his fingers replace the washcloth in his exploration. They moved up to my breasts before he squeezed them and molded them to his palms. He then pinched my nipples and started kissing my neck. I groaned as his fingers slipped in between my legs and he caressed my clit in the water. The feeling was intense and slightly different.

After a few minutes, I shifted in the bathtub so that I was straddling him. He took my breast in his mouth, and I reached down and held his cock still so that I could ride him. We both groaned as I slid down on his hardness in the water and started gyrating. My movements were stilted in the small space, but he used his hands to hold my ass and push me up and down on his cock. Our breathing was fast as we fucked in the bathtub and the water splashed over the side as we orgasmed together. I lay flat on him and he held me for a few minutes as our bodies continued trembling against each other.

"I think it's time for me to wash you again," he said softly and kissed my cheek as his hand grabbed the washcloth again. I shook my head and took it out of his hand.

"No, I think it's time for me to wash you." I smiled at him deviously and lowered the washcloth to his cock.

We left the bathtub about thirty minutes later and made love one more time before lying next to each other in the bed. I felt tired and confused. My heart was playing games with my head and I didn't know which side was up.

"I've really missed you, Katie," Brandon mumbled as he played with my breasts in bed. "I think about fucking your brains out all the time."

His words sparked something in me, and as I rolled out of the bed, Brandon sat up.

"Where are you going?" he mumbled as he reached for me.

"I'm going home." I stood there in front of him in all of my naked glory, feeling powerful and satiated.

"What?" His eyes narrowed, and he ran his hand through his hair before rubbing his chin. "Where are you going?"

"Back to my hotel room." I gave him a wide smile and then bent down to kiss him one last time. As I pulled away, I let my breasts rub against his arm and I pulled away quickly as his hand went to grasp my left breast.

"You can't go now," he groaned. "You're drunk. It's not safe."

"I'm not eighteen anymore, Brandon. I can handle my

106

wine." I laughed and pulled on my dress. "I think I'll be fine getting home by myself."

"No." He jumped up and walked over to me. "I'm not going to let you leave."

"I don't think you get it, Brandon." I pulled on my shoes. "I'm not a damsel in distress, and I don't need you. Thanks for the fuck though. You taught me some new tricks." I smiled at him as I grabbed my handbag. "I think Matt will appreciate all the skills you've taught me when we finally get to make love."

His face turned murderous at my words, and I walked past him quickly, hoping to get out of his apartment with the last word.

I felt high as I hurried to the door. I had done it. I had fucked him and now I was leaving him without a clue as to what was going on. I had taken what I wanted and now I was the one in control. I'd showed him that he meant as little to me as I meant to him. My hand reached for the front doorknob and I grinned to myself in excitement. This was match point and I was about to win. I had done it.

A second later, I felt his hands on my shoulders.

"What are you doing?"

I gasped as he pushed me against the door and moved in against me. He raised his arms above my shoulders and leaned against me, pressing me into the door, his body acting like a trap.

"I just told you, Katie. I'm not going to let you leave." His eyes glittered down at me and his hand slipped up my thigh through the slit in my dress. His fingers pushed their way in between my legs and worked their way into my wetness, rubbing against my clit before slowly entering me. My body betrayed me by buckling at his touch and my legs moved apart involuntarily as he fucked me with his fingers. "And I don't think you want to leave right now, do you?" he whispered against my whimpering lips.

I closed my eyes as my sudden and swift climax

answered him. And once again he was in control.

***

"Good morning, sleepyhead." Brandon's smiling face was staring down at me as I woke up. I stretched in the bed and yawned.

"It's too dark out to be morning," I groaned and closed my eyes again.

"It's not too early for morning sex though." His hand crept up from my stomach to my right breast and I moaned as he pinched my nipple.

"Brandon." I rolled over toward him. "Not right now."

"I guess I'll give you a break." He laughed and pulled me toward him. "I guess we did wear ourselves out last night."

"Yeah." I smiled back at him and kissed him softly before freezing. This wasn't a dream. This was real life. I was in bed with Brandon still. Flashbacks of the night before came back to me—my trying to leave, his stopping me and fingering me to one of the most intense orgasms I had ever had. Going back to bed and making love again before falling asleep.

"I'm glad you decided to stay last night." His eyes glinted into mine.

"I didn't have much of a choice, did I?" I pulled away from him.

"You always have a choice."

"I wanted to leave last night."

"To go home and call Matt?" His eyes narrowed. "Were you going to tell him how you fucked me again, but it was all good because you were going to let him fuck you next, like some sort of sloppy seconds?"

"How dare you!" I slapped his face hard and then clapped my hand to my mouth in shock as I stared at the bright red fingerprints across his face. "Oh my God, I'm sorry."

"No. I deserved it." He lay back and sighed. "I should apologize."

"No, it's fine." I shook my head and lay back as well. "It was my bad. I wanted to get a rise out of you last night. I guess I was trying to play a game and it didn't go the way I planned."

"So you didn't really want to go?"

"I don't know." I shrugged and looked away.

"Maria and I have never had sex," Brandon blurted out, and he turned toward me with intense eyes.

"What?" I turned back toward him.

"We've never had sex." He laughed. "I know that's hard to believe."

"But you're engaged?" I stared at him, confused. "I don't get it."

"I did it to help her." He shrugged. "I can't really talk about it."

"Do you love her?" I whispered, yelling at myself for asking the question that plagued my heart.

"I don't love her." He shook his head.

"Oh." I stared at him with wide eyes. Where did this leave us? Was it possible that we had a future?

"I've missed you, Katie." He leaned in toward me, and his fingers ran through my hair and down my face.

"I've missed you as well." I reached over and ran my fingers along his lips. "I've thought about your face for so long. I can't believe I'm here with you right now."

"I need to have you again. I need to feel myself in you." He grabbed me and pulled me toward him. "Let me love you, Katie."

I nodded and he pulled me up onto my knees before getting behind me.

"I remember that you always used to love doggy style." He laughed as he positioned his already hard cock next to my dripping opening. "I can go so deep from behind. It almost feels like we are becoming one."

"I know." I groaned as he entered me. "Oh, Brandon.

Don't stop." I groaned again as he slowly slid in and out of me. "Please go faster."

"Do you trust me, Katie?" His hands gripped my hips as he increased his pace slightly.

"Yes," I moaned and closed my eyes as I fell forward slowly.

"Let me take you in a way I've never taken you before." He grunted and I cried out as he withdrew his cock from me.

"What are you doing?" I moaned, wanting to feel him inside of me.

"I took one of your cherries. Let me take the other one too."

"What?" My jaw dropped open and I froze.

"Let me love you, Katie." His thumb grazed my butthole and I jumped.

"I don't know." I shook my head and turned to look at his face. I watched as he took his thumb and sucked it. Then he lowered it back to my asshole and rubbed it gently. He rubbed my asshole and then down to my clit and back. My legs buckled every time he touched my clit and my nerves were on high alert as his thumb trailed back and forth.

I didn't say anything as he continued teasing me. He then reached his fingers in between my legs and his fingers played with my clit before entering me. I groaned as I felt a small orgasm shake my body. He withdrew his fingers and rubbed his cock with my juices. He pushed me forward and rubbed the tip of his cock along my slit to my butthole. I groaned as his cock rubbed against my clit and I pushed back into him, hoping he would enter me.

"Hold on, sweet pea." He kept teasing me. Then I felt the tip of him at the other entry. I froze as he slowly entered me. It was a weird and different feeling. I felt strangely aroused by the feel of him in a place I'd never had a man before. He groaned as he slid into me slowly.

"Fuck, it's so tight," he muttered, and I felt myself

grow wetter at how turned on he sounded. "Oh, Katie. Fuck. I'm going to come." He moved faster and faster, and I gripped the bed sheets as he stole my anal cherry.

"Oh, Katie!" He shouted my name as he pulled out of me and entered my pussy again. "Oh, fuck," He groaned as he slammed into me, his fingers holding my hips tightly against him as he fucked me hard. "Oh, yes." His body shuddered as he came hard and fast, pulling out of me and spilling his cum on my ass and legs.

I collapsed flat on the bed and he pulled me into his arms as he spooned me. I fell asleep with a small smile on my face, feeling sore and happy. *He's never had sex with Maria,* I sang to myself. *He can't love her if they've never had sex.* And then I fell asleep.

The phone rang and woke me up, but I didn't open my eyes. I felt content and happy as I lay in his bed. I was hopeful for the future now. Maybe we really had a chance. I had given myself to him freely and let him do things to me that I would never have let anyone else I didn't trust do. Deep in my heart I knew that everything was going to be okay. Everything had worked out for the best. My perfectly orchestrated idea had gone according to plan.

"Maria, what's going on?" he whispered into the phone, and I peeked at him through my lashes. "No, I'm not busy." His words hurt me as I lay there, but I tried not to feel jealous. He didn't love her. He hadn't even slept with her. I had nothing to be jealous of. I had just given myself to him, trusted him. He would do the right thing.

"What happened to Harry?" His voice was sharp. "Oh my God," he gasped. "No, it's okay. I'm the boss. I'll explain. I'll be on the first plane home. Just tell him that Daddy is on the way. Give him a big hug and kiss from me." And then he hung up. I sat up then, my heart beating and my head pounding.

"What's going on?" I spoke up, and he looked at me in surprise.

"I've got to go. My son is in the hospital."

"Your son?" My face paled as I stared at him.

"Yes, my son." He turned away from me and started pulling on clothes.

"I don't understand," I spoke softly, but I wanted to scream, *I thought you told me you never had sex with her.*

"What don't you understand?" His voice was annoyed. "I'm not a monk. I had sex. I wasn't wearing a condom. My sperm swam. I now have a child."

"But you said..." My words drifted off as he threw my dress at me.

"Get ready. We have to leave." He walked out of the room, and I stood up slowly, my heart breaking and my asshole a sore reminder of how once again he had screwed me over.

I slowly pulled on my dress and my shoes. I felt numb inside and out. This was worse than before. This time I felt like I would never get over the pain. I was forever ruined by this man, this man that I both loved and hated.

"Come on, Katie," he called out to me from the front door. "Let's go."

He drove me back to the hotel in silence and I jumped out of the car in a hurry, feeling like the world was about to end.

"Thanks for last night, Katie," he called out to me as I walked away. "It meant a lot to me." I increased my pace as I hurried into the hotel, and it took everything in me to not turn around and tell him to fuck off when he told me he would call me.

CHAPTER 4

Meg felt awful that I had stayed in San Francisco because of her losing her job. She knew as soon as I arrived back looking like the creature from the Black Lagoon that something was wrong. My eyes were bloodshot and I hadn't even bothered combing my hair. I knew that I'd looked like a mess on the airplane, but I just didn't care.

As I walked into the apartment and collapsed onto the floor in tears, I felt like my life was over. I'd only felt this way twice before, and both of those heartbreaks had been due to Brandon as well.

"Oh my God, Katie." Meg ran into the living room and fell to the floor to hold me. "What's wrong?"

"It was horrible," I sobbed. "Worse than I thought it was going to be."

"So he recognized you?" Meg's eyes looked worried.

"Yes." I nodded. "Right away."

"That's good then, right?"

"He was going to propose to me!" I cried, the tears escaping me fast and furiously now as my body shook.

"What?" Meg looked shocked. "This weekend?"

"No, silly." I stopped crying long enough to laugh for a few seconds. "He was going to propose the Christmas we broke up."

"Oh, wow. I'm sorry, Katie." She hugged me close to her. "That must have been hard to hear."

"I slept with him," I burst out. "And it was wonderful and I thought he still loved me, but I don't know that he ever really did."

"What? Of course he loved you."

"He's engaged." I jumped up and hit my hands against the wall. "He's engaged and I still slept with him. I feel so dirty. I can't believe I let him hurt me like this again."

"It's not your fault." Meg didn't try to stop me from hitting the wall, but rather she stood there waiting for the moment she needed to hug me again. "Did you tell him about...you know?" Her voice trailed off, and her words ignited more pain in my chest. A pain that had been long buried and we never spoke about. I shook my head slightly and turned toward her.

"I don't know how I'm going to face him at work tomorrow. I don't know what I'm going to do!" I cried out. "I hate him, Meg. He used me. He made me feel cheap. Even cheaper than when he dumped me outside Butler Library. I know I lied, but I didn't do it maliciously. I didn't do it to hurt him."

"He's obviously got other issues, Katie. I mean, he is starting to sound like a bit of a psycho. Let's be real here—you never really knew him. You didn't even date for a year. It was a whirlwind relationship. He was your first love, and he's turned out to be a jerk."

"Why would he treat me like this?" I sobbed. "He has a son."

"Oh." Meg's eyes widened and she held my hand.

"He told me he never even had sex with his fiancée, but they have a kid."

"Are you sure it's hers?"

"She's the one who called him and told him that his son was in the hospital. As soon as she called, he forgot about me. He dismissed me like I was nothing. And then he casually thanked me for the fuck."

"Oh, Katie." She shook her head. "If you don't want to go back, you don't have to. We'll figure something out. If I've got to break into my trip fund, I will."

"No." I shook my head vehemently. "You've been working on that fund since you were ten years old. I'm not going to let you use that money on rent."

"I'd rather do that than have you face him one more time."

I squared my shoulders and wiped my tears away while taking a few deep breaths. "Thank you, Meg." I squeezed her hands. "I'll see how I feel in a few days."

"So you're not going back to work?"

"Not tomorrow, I'm not." I sighed. "Let him fire me if he wants. I'm going to get in the shower now."

"Okay. I'll be out here if you need to talk."

"Thanks, but I'm feeling pretty tired. I'll probably just go to bed."

"I'm going to start looking for new jobs right away, and not just law jobs. I'll take anything. Just so we can pay our rent."

"Thanks, Meg." I smiled at her gratefully and walked to the shower in defeat. It was over. It was definitely over. Every hope and wish I'd had in the last seven years was gone. Brandon Hastings and I were never going to get back together again. I slipped my clothes off and got into the shower, allowing the scalding hot water to burn my back and hopefully wash some of my sins away. There were so many things I regretted about our history together. So many little pieces I would have changed. I thought back to his phone call and started crying again. He had a son. A baby boy that was probably his pride and joy. A child he loved with all his heart. A child who came first in his life. And it broke me. After everything, it was the news that he had a child that finally broke me down.

***

"Hello, can I speak to Ms. Raymond please?" a snooty voice asked as I picked up the phone.

"Speaking." I sat up in my bed and put the ice cream tub to the side, not wanting it to fall over while I was on the phone.

"Ms. Raymond, this is Priscilla calling from Marathon Corporation's HR department. You haven't been to work in three days, and you haven't called in, so we wanted to make sure that everything was okay."

"I'm fine."

"Then why are you not at work, Ms. Raymond?" Her voice was harsh, and I knew that if she could she would fire me on the spot.

"I don't know what to say," I replied honestly and laughed about what her reaction would be if I told her the truth. *I slept with the CEO, who's my ex, found out he was engaged and has a son, and he broke my heart again. Oh yeah, and I also let him fuck my asshole. Win for me.*

"Will you be coming in tomorrow, Ms. Raymond?"

"Doubt it." I grabbed my spoon and dug into my Ben & Jerry's. I needed a strawberry cheesecake ice cream fix.

"Ms. Raymond, I have to tell you that—" She paused, and I heard some whispering in the background. "One moment please."

"Katie." His voice was silky and smooth, and my heart flipped.

"Brandon," I replied softly, the ice cream in my spoon long forgotten as it dripped onto the bed.

"What are you doing?"

"Eating ice cream," I replied automatically and he laughed.

"Come into work tomorrow please."

"I can't." My voice shook.

"I need you on my team, Katie. Please come into work tomorrow."

"You hurt me," I whispered. "I don't want to see you again."

"Fight for it, Katie." His voice was urgent. "You worked so hard to get this job. Are you really going to throw it away?"

"I don't know what to do. I hate you."

"Think about what you really want." He paused and then continued. "Think about what's in your heart and fight for it. Don't just walk away again."

"What are you talking about?" My tone grew angry.

"I hope to see you tomorrow." His voice was soft now. "I hope you're the warrior princess I always thought you were." And then he hung up.

I lay back on the bed with my eyes wide and my heart beating fast. I was shivering even though it wasn't cold. I closed my eyes as I remembered the last time he had called me his warrior princess.

It had been a Saturday, and we'd gone to lunch at some cute chic restaurant in Soho. We'd shared a salad and a sandwich and had been playing footsie under the table. I'd been going on about some new book I'd read. I think it was *A Tale of Two Cities* by Charles Dickens, so it wasn't actually new—just new for me. I had never really studied much history, so I had been fascinated by the history of relations between France and England.

Brandon was a bit of a history buff, so he'd been telling me about Louis the Fourteenth and his wife Marie Antoinette when I saw the manager of the restaurant run outside and start berating two young boys who were going through the trash can at the curb. The two boys looked tattered and dirty and had taken food out of the trash can to eat. Without thinking, I jumped up and ran outside.

"What's going on?" I asked the manager and noticed that one of the boys was crying.

"These two thieves are going through the trash. They need to leave."

"Thieves? They look like they're seven or eight." I shook my head. "And they are stealing rotten food. I bet they're hungry. Are you boys hungry?" I gave them both a warm smile and they nodded slowly. "You should be giving them something to eat, not chasing them off." I glared at the manager.

"I'm not encouraging these hoodrats."

"Everyone is a human being and should be treated with dignity and respect." I glared at him, my voice getting louder.

"What's going on out here?" Brandon's arm slid around my shoulder and his voice sounded concerned.

"These two boys were going through the trash for food because they're hungry and he won't let them take the scraps." My voice was passionate. "I think he should be getting them food from the kitchen and he's not even letting them take the food in the garbage."

"I have a business to run. I can't feed every Tom, Dick, and Harry for free." He glared back at me.

"These are kids."

"I don't care." He turned around and walked back into the restaurant.

"Wait here with the boys." I looked at Brandon and then hurried back into the restaurant. "I'd like to order four sandwiches with four bags of potato chips, four cookies, and four bottles of water." I marched up to the manager. "And I want them STAT."

"Excuse me?"

"If you don't want me to start shouting and letting everyone know how greedy and uncharitable this restaurant is, you will get them ready now." I spoke calmly. "Don't worry. I'll pay for the food."

He stared at me for a few seconds but then turned around and put in the orders. I smiled to myself at my small victory and walked back outside with the bags of food as soon as I had them. The boys had huge smiles on their faces as they stood there with Brandon and even wider smiles when I handed them the food.

"Thank you." They grinned at me and Brandon and then ran off down the road. I watched them with slight worry. What was going to happen to them once the food was gone?

"You got them food." Brandon pulled me toward him. "I'm so proud to be with you, Katie. You spoke up for those boys like a warrior princess and then you went back and got them food. You're everything I want to be when I grow up."

"Oh, Brandon." I giggled as he kissed me. "I guess reading this book about inequality in France all those years ago and witnessing how it still goes on has gotten to me. Little kids shouldn't be searching for food in the streets. There is something wrong with that in a country where we have so much and people are literally throwing good food away. Yet those two boys aren't even allowed to rummage for the leftovers. It's wrong."

"I completely agree." He kissed the top of my head. "Never change, Katie. Never stop being my warrior princess."

I sat up in bed as I remembered that day. I'd been a different girl back then. I'd been fearless. I had believed that nothing could or would stop me from achieving all of my dreams. My life had changed after Brandon broke up with me. But it wasn't his fault that I had lost a part of myself. I had made those decisions. I was the one who was in charge of my destiny and life. And he was right. I had worked hard in college and grad school to get a job like this. Granted, this particular company had offered extra perks, but I still wanted it.

I still needed to prove myself. I had let Brandon win the game once before. I wasn't going to let him win again and kick me off the board. I jumped off the bed and walked to my closet. I was going to go back to work. I was going to leave all my personal feelings at home. I was going to show Brandon that I was the warrior princess he let get away.

***

Life is a funny thing. I went back to work the next day and Brandon wasn't even there. All the pep talks I had given myself hadn't even been needed. I'd felt tense almost all of the day until my immediate boss told me that Brandon was out of town. I didn't ask where or why or with whom. I was starting to realize that the less information I knew, the better it would be for me.

The next day he wasn't there either, and then it was the weekend. By the time the next Monday rolled around, I was feeling more confident and sure of myself. Maybe he felt bad about what he had done and I would never have to see him again.

"Yeah, yeah, yeah," I sang along with the song on the radio that one of the secretaries was playing as I went through the sales figures from the previous week.

"Good morning, Katie." Three simple words stopped my heart. I looked up slowly and my eyes gobbled him in. He looked so smart and debonair in his navy pinstripe suit with his crisp white shirt.

"Good morning, Brandon." I nodded and smiled quickly. He walked into my office and closed the door.

"It's good to see you." His eyes surveyed my face, but I wasn't sure what he was looking for.

"It's good to be back. Sales are going great. Thirty-five percent increase over last year." I mumbled on about work, hoping that we would keep it professional.

"I noticed." He sat down in the seat in front of my desk. "You're doing a great job."

"I'm trying." I nodded and looked down. "How is your son?" I groaned inwardly as the words slipped out. Why was I doing this to myself?

"He's fine." His eyes shone brightly. "Thanks for asking. He fell off his bike and hurt his knee. Maria overreacted and took him to the hospital." He shrugged. "I guess her maternal instinct kicked in."

"I see." My heart broke at his words. He was finally admitting it. Maria was Harry's mother, so that meant that

Maria and he'd had sex. He had lied to me. I stared at him and I wanted to shout, *How could you lie to me like that?* So easily. It burned in me that he had no shame about it and I realized that must have been the way he felt with me. Only a lot worse.

"He's a good boy." He stared at me intently. "A very handsome boy too. He has his mother's eyes and my hair." He laughed. "There's no mistaking he's my kid."

"Why's that?" I smiled weakly. "Because he's so handsome?"

"No, because he's into everything." He laughed. "He wants to know everything and do everything."

"He sounds like a good kid."

"He's the best. He's my life."

"You and Maria are very lucky to have him in your life."

"We are." He nodded and stood up. "I should let you get back to work. Come to my office around 11:30 a.m. I need to discuss some things with you."

"Sure." I nodded in agreement as he walked out the door.

"Oh, and Katie." He turned around and gave me a small smile. "I'm glad you came back."

I smiled to myself as he walked out of the room. I could handle this. Yes, the pain of hearing him talk about his son killed me inside, but I wasn't going to die. Eventually, it would get better. And I'd be able to work with him without always thinking of the what-ifs.

My phone rang then, and I grabbed it up without looking at the screen. "Hello?"

"Katie, where have you been? I've been worried sick about you!"

"Oh, Matt." I bit my lower lip. "Sorry, I've been busy with work."

"I haven't seen you in close to two weeks." His voice was accusing. "Can I take you out to dinner tonight?"

"Dinner?" I repeated weakly.

"Yes," he laughed. "It's what most boyfriends do every once in a while."

"Funny." I faked a laugh. "I guess dinner would be fine."

"Don't sound so enthusiastic!"

"Sorry, just been busy."

"I see. Well, I wanted to celebrate my promotion."

"Promotion?"

"Yeah."

"At the *Wall Street Journal*?"

"That is where I've been reporting for the last three years."

"Sorry, sorry." I rubbed my forehead. "I'm a little distracted. Congratulations. That is great news."

"So dinner and drinks?"

"Sure."

"Maybe we can go back to my place after and watch a movie." His voice was light. "And see where the night takes us."

"I guess so." I bit back a sigh. This was getting harder and harder.

"I'll see you tonight then. I'll text you the restaurant info."

"Sounds good."

"See you later, Katie."

I hung up and stared at the phone, feeling guilty. I felt awful about playing Matt, and I knew that I needed to break up with him. Dating him wasn't right and it wasn't fair. Especially seeing as I had essentially used him. Maybe that was why it had all blown up in my face. I'd been using people and lying for months. Even Meg didn't know the truth. I sighed and went back to the files. I was going to have to come clean and move on. I would dedicate my life to my job. That was all I had left right now.

***

"Hey." I walked into his office without knocking.

"Have a seat," he pointed to a chair and whispered as he was on the phone. "Bill, I understand that you think that Epsonal is worth five million, but I'm telling you it's overpriced. I will give you two million and allow you to keep a one percent equity share in the company, and that's only because I'm being a nice guy." He paused. "I have to go now, so think about it. You have twenty-four hours to accept or decline my offer." He hung up the phone and smiled at me. "Sorry about that."

"Are you trying to buy Epsonal, the electronics company?" I asked, frowning slightly.

"Yes, why?" He looked at me in interest.

"What you said was wrong. The company is worth at least twenty million—or at least it will be in a few weeks when the government awards them the military contract," I answered before realizing I had slipped up. I wasn't supposed to know about the military contract. No one was supposed to know. I only knew because I had seen the files on Matt's computer when I had been looking for something else.

"How did you know about the contract?" Brandon's eyes narrowed. "No one is supposed to know about that. Bill, the CEO of the company, doesn't even know."

"And you're using that lack of information to buy his company from him early." I shook my head in shock. "So you can get it cheap."

"That's how business works." He shrugged.

"But that's illegal. That's inside information." My mouth dropped open. "That's wrong."

"It can't be that inside if you've read about it somewhere." His eyes challenged me and I kept my mouth shut. There was no way I was going to tell him that I read it while snooping around in my reporter boyfriend's laptop.

"What did you want to see me about?" I changed the subject.

"I wanted to let you know that I am going to need you to start working nights." He leafed through some files. "You're the best manager I have right now and I need to work with you on some important projects."

"Okay." I swallowed hard as he undid the knot of his tie and pulled it off.

"Excuse me. There are some days that ties make me feel like I'm suffocating."

"No worries." I smiled weakly and watched as he pulled his jacket off as well. I watched as his chest muscles flexed beneath his shirt and shifted in my seat. He was so sexy. Just staring at him turned me on.

"I have a business trip planned for next weekend that I need you to come on."

"Oh?"

"It's in London." He smiled as I gasped. "I know you've always wanted to go."

"Are you sure you need me to go?"

"Yes." He nodded. "I'm very sure."

"I'll try and make it work then."

"Apologize to your boyfriend, Tom. I hope I'm not ruining any plans."

"His name is Matt, and no, you're not."

"Good." Brandon stood up, walked to his office door, slammed it shut, and locked it before walking back over to me.

"What are you doing?" I whispered as he stood in front of me, unbuttoning his shirt.

"Disrobing." He grinned and threw it on the ground.

"But why? I thought you told me to come because you needed to discuss something with me?"

"I do. I need to discuss how hot you are and how my cock is aching to fuck you."

"What?" My face heated up as my hand ran to his chest.

"I know you want me too." He pulled me up. "You can't deny the unbelievable chemistry we have, Katie."

124

"We shouldn't do this, Brandon." I shook my head and gasped as he grabbed my hand and placed it over his already hard cock.

"I'm hard just from looking at you. I need to be inside of you," he growled and his lips came down on mine softly, waiting to see how I would react. I was too weak, I couldn't resist him and I kissed him back passionately, opening my mouth to let his tongue in and sucking on it.

His hands worked their way under my skirt and he pulled it up so that it was sitting on my waist. His fingers slipped between my legs and rubbed me through my panties. I groaned at his touch and traced my fingers down his back and to his ass.

"Oh, Katie, I can never get enough of you," he groaned and ripped open my blouse, burying his head in the valley between my breasts before nudging my left bra cup to the side with his nose and then devouring my nipple. I moaned as my body arched towards him and he moved me back slightly and lifted me onto the desk.

I leaned forward, grabbed his belt, and pulled him towards me. His eyes darkened as I undid his buckle and unzipped him. His cock sprang out hard and proud, and desire sprung through me. I couldn't stop myself from running my fingers along his shaft and teasing him. I couldn't keep my hands off this man. Our sexual chemistry was too great. I closed my eyes as he pushed me back onto the desk and pulled my panties down to my knees.

"Sex in the office never gets old, does it?" he growled down at me as his fingers rubbed me gently. I moaned as he fingered me and then lifted my legs up to his shoulders. He pulled my ass down to the edge of the table and then slowly entered me. His cock drove into me slowly and his finger rubbed my clit as he slid in and out of me. I groaned at his touch—it felt too good, too intense. My body could barely stand how sweet the pleasure was that was building up in me.

"You feel so good." Brandon's voice was tense as he

increased his pace. "Your pussy was made for me. Each time I make love to you, it welcomes me back with pleasure." His eyes glittered down on me. "I could get used to these office fucks." His hands reached up to squeeze my breasts and I held on to the table as he started moving faster and faster. "Oh, Katie. Fuck. I'm going to come." He groaned and my body started to orgasm in response to his words.

BANG BANG. The loud knocks on the door made us both freeze.

"Who is it?" Brandon's went still, his cock still in me as he paused.

"Daddy, it's me, Harry," a little voice spoke up and I sat up in horror. Brandon made a face before he quickly pulled up his pants and grabbed up his shirt.

"Just a minute, son," he called out and pushed me to the other side of the table. "Go under the table. Now," he commanded me and I ran quickly and hid under the table while Brandon quickly got dressed again.

"Daddy," Harry's little voice called out as he banged on the door again. "Let me in."

"Be patient, Harry. I'm coming." Brandon's voice sounded loving and patient as I listened to him throwing on his clothes over the loud beating of my heart.

"Daddy." The voice carried into the room as Brandon opened the door. "You took forever."

"Sorry. I was just finishing up something."

"We came to take you to lunch." The boy giggled. "And I want a burger."

"What do you say?"

"Please."

"Don't forget your manners, Harry." Brandon's voice was soft. "And I guess I can make time for a burger."

"Yay!" Harry ran up to the desk and my heart stopped still. What if he decided to sit in his dad's chair? What if he saw me?

"Come, Harry. Sit on the couch," Brandon called over

to him, and I heard the boy's footsteps retreat.

"Can I get a toy today as well, please, Daddy?"

"We'll see."

"And some ice cream?" the boy continued, and I wanted to laugh. I also really wanted to see what Brandon's son looked like. His mini-me. His child. It made my heart ache, but I still wanted to see. I guess I wanted to torment myself with what could have been.

"Now, now, Harry. Don't you think that's expecting a bit much?" Brandon's voice was light and I could tell that he was amused.

"No."

"There you are, Harry." A female voice carried through the room and my heart stopped.

"Maria." Brandon sounded happy and not like someone who had nearly been busted cheating. "I was wondering where you were."

"You know your son." She laughed. "As soon as he's in the building, he's rushing to Daddy's office, and he doesn't care who he leaves behind."

"Sorry." Harry laughed and then mumbled something I couldn't hear.

"Shall we go then?" Brandon laughed. "I'm feeling hungry myself right now. Let's go get something to eat."

"Yay." Harry squealed and I heard him run out of the room. Then a few seconds later the door closed. I waited for about two minutes before I crawled out from under the desk and straightened my clothes. There were no tears left for me to cry, though once again I felt ashamed of myself. My heart felt heavy as I walked to the door and I knew what I had to do. I had to leave Marathon Corporation. There was no way I was going to be able to work with him and be okay. I had made my bed and now I had to get out. If I ever wanted to regain my sanity, I needed to get out now.

CHAPTER 5

"I'm not sure why you ever dated Matt," Meg said as she walked with me to the subway station.

"He's a nice enough guy." I sighed, feeling guilty. Meg didn't know the whole story, and I was ashamed of myself for keeping secrets from her.

"I know. He seemed nice," she agreed. "He just didn't seem like the sort of guy you go for."

"What guys?" I rolled my eyes. "Matt's the only other guy I've really dated, besides Brandon."

"I know, and it's time for you to finally move on." Meg stopped and turned toward me. "I don't want you to hate me for saying this, but I need to say it. What happened wasn't your fault. Yes, you lied, and yes, you were a dumbass, but you were eighteen. You made a mistake. You did what you thought you had to do. You were in school, Katie. Your life was just starting. I know it hurts like hell, and I can't imagine what pain you're going through, but you can't keep beating yourself up. You need to move on. Please, for the sake of your sanity, you need to move on."

"I know." I smiled at her gently. I knew how hard it was for her to talk to me like this. She'd been with me after the breakup and she was the only one who knew everything I'd gone through, everything I'd lost when the relationship had ended.

"I hope Matt doesn't cry when you dump him." Meg made a face to lighten the mood.

"That would be bad." I laughed. "But I think he'll be fine."

"And you're handing in your resignation tomorrow as well?"

"Yeah." I nodded my head assertively. "I need to move on, but I also need to be professional about it. I can't just sit in my room and pretend that life isn't still going on, just because I'm depressed."

"I'm proud of you."

"I couldn't do this without you." I squeezed her hands gratefully. "I'm so upset that we have to rely on your savings.

"Don't even think about it." She shook her head. "That's what best friends are for. I'll make more money. I'll be able to go on a trip another time."

"I love you, Meg."

"I love you too, Katie." She gave me a quick hug. "Now go break up with Matt gently while I go and try to get a job."

"Good luck." I grinned at her. "You'll be a shoo-in for the bartender job."

"Let's hope so." She groaned. "At this point, we just need money."

"You got this."

"Thanks, luv. See you later."

"Bye." I watched her hurrying down the street and said a quick prayer for her. She was hoping to get this part-time bartender job that had been advertised at the laundromat. The pay was great, and no experience was needed. If she got it, it would definitely help us as we both looked for new jobs. I took a deep breath and ran down to catch the train. This was it. My old life was about to end, and my new one was ready to begin.

***

I didn't have the heart to break up with Matt over dinner. It just seemed too cruel to congratulate him on his promotion and then dump him in the next breath. I decided to do it in his apartment, and then I'd come clean about everything. I wanted him to know what I had done and why, so he could understand that he had done nothing wrong. The reason I was ending things wasn't because I no longer liked him. It was because I was still in love with someone else.

We walked into his apartment and I watched as Matt hurried into the kitchen to get a bottle of wine. He seemed like he was excited, and I had a bad feeling that he thought that tonight was going to be the night that we consummated our relationship.

He brought back two glasses of red wine and I took mine eagerly. I was going to need liquid courage to get me through the night.

"What movie do you want to watch?" He shifted closer to me on the couch and I tried not to recoil.

"Actually, I was hoping we could talk." I took a deep breath and he frowned at me.

"Sure, but what do you want to talk about?"

"It's over, Matt. I can't go out with you anymore," I blurted out, and I was surprised that his face remained the same. Even the expression in his eyes didn't look shocked or upset.

"I see." He nodded and sipped some more wine. "Why is that?"

I took a deep breath and let it out. "About seven years ago, I dated a guy. A successful businessman. I loved him, but things went wrong. I waited for him to come back to me and he never did. I tried to forget him, but I couldn't." I chewed on my lower lip as I continued on with my story. "About a year ago, I decided that I was going to try to see him again. Maybe get close to him, see if any of the old feelings were there. I wanted to see if we could give the relationship another go."

"Okay."

"I didn't want it to be a one-off encounter." I sighed. "I wanted us to be around each other. I wanted to see if perhaps we could make it work. So I started trying researching him. I found a lot of articles about him. Business stuff, you know? And I realized that the best way for me to get back into his life would be if I went to work for him. But I knew that he liked to flip companies. I knew I had to get in with a company before he did, so it wouldn't look suspicious. So I needed to get a contact, someone who knew a lot about business."

"And that's where I came in?" Matt raised an eyebrow and I nodded.

"Most of the articles I read about him were written by you. You seemed to have information that others didn't." I bit my lip. "So I orchestrated a meeting in the lobby of your office building."

"The classic woman-bumps-into-man-and-spills-coffee-on-him routine." He spoke slowly as he remembered our first encounter.

"I didn't mean to use you," I sighed. "I wanted to be friends, but you were so nice and it just kind of became a dating thing."

"So you used me for information?"

"I looked through your files on your computer." I nodded. "I saw a list of companies that you said this businessman was thinking of purchasing." I looked down at my lap, embarrassed and not wanting to say Brandon's name. "And I applied to all of them for jobs."

"So my information was right?" Matt asked eagerly, and I wanted to laugh.

"Yeah. I got jobs at three of the companies. I chose my position based on an article you were writing. I knew then which company he was buying, so I accepted the job. And I started working there a month before it was even announced that he was buying the corporation. It worked out perfectly. Even my best friend didn't know that I had taken the job there because I wanted to see him again." I closed my eyes as guilt racked my body. "But it didn't work out. It was a mistake. I shouldn't have done what I did. And I'm sorry. I'm really sorry if I've hurt you."

"I can't say that it feels great." His eyes were blank. "I never expected this."

"I'm leaving my job as well," I hurried out so that he knew that it had all blown up in my face. "I'm quitting tomorrow."

"What?" This time his voice rose and he looked worried. "You can't quit your job."

"I have to." I nodded and I jumped up as I felt myself becoming emotional. "I can't work with this man anymore. He's horrible. I can't do it. I'm quitting and I'm never looking back."

"Katie, please. I think you need to think about this." Matt jumped up as well and I could see worry in his eyes. "You seem to love this job. You can't just quit."

"I can and I am." I leaned over and kissed his cheek. "I need to go home now. I'm sorry. But I have to go." I hurried to the front door and opened it, feeling awful. My insides were churning with guilt and I rested my head against the door.

Matt had looked awful right before I'd left. He'd looked like his world was about to cave in, and that was because of me. I couldn't believe how badly I had treated him. And for what? I shook my head and sighed.

I had to go back and explain to him that it wasn't his fault. I didn't want him to hate me. I wanted him to know that there were things I had really liked about him. I didn't want to leave the apartment with Matt feeling like he'd been used. I'd felt that way before, and I knew how horrible it was.

I walked back toward the living room to apologize once again for how everything had gone, but he wasn't there. I walked slowly toward the bedroom, half afraid that I would see him crying or something. I knew he was a man, but I'd never really witnessed how emotional men did or didn't get at the end of a relationship.

I reached the door of his bedroom and stood in the open doorway. Matt's back was to me, and I reached to knock on the door to alert him of my presence when he pulled out his phone and dialed some numbers. I decided to wait until he was done with the call and just stood there for a moment.

"Mr. Hastings, please." His voice was worried and slightly urgent as he spoke. "Hey, Brandon. It's Matt. We have a problem."

BOOK 3
PROLOGUE

He watched them as he'd been asked to, snapping photograph after photograph. They looked happy and in love. This was one assignment that made him satisfied. She was a good girl: sweet, innocent, smart, and real. She wasn't a gold digger like all the others, and that made him happy.

His phone rang and he answered it eagerly; he was always excited when one of his sons called.

"Dad, I wanted to know if you want to come to dinner tonight? We're going to try out the new Italian place on Amsterdam."

"Sure, I'll be finished with work in about an hour." He turned the ignition in his car as he watched the couple leave the restaurant. "But I gotta go now. I'll see you later, Matt."

He hung up before his son could answer and put his camera on the seat. He couldn't afford to lose them tonight. Mr. Hastings had been very clear in his instructions. He smiled to himself as he thought about the money he was going to receive for the assignment. He looked down at the passenger seat to make sure that the envelope was still there. He would drop it off before going to dinner. Mr. Hastings would have the information to read in the morning. And then he could make his own decisions about what to do.

CHAPTER 1
KATIE

I stepped back into the corridor with my heart pounding. Why was Matt calling Brandon? He didn't know Brandon. Brandon didn't know him. It just didn't make sense to me. What was going on here? I knew I had two choices: I could go and confront Matt and ask him what was going on, or I could pretend I didn't know anything and try to find out the information another way. I stood in the corridor and thought for a moment. Clearly, Brandon knew Matt and Matt knew Brandon. Which meant that Brandon had been playing me from the beginning of my trip to San Francisco. He had used Matt to gain information on me. I didn't know when he had found out about Matt, but I did know that all his questions about my boyfriend were false. Which meant that he was playing me. He had deliberately tried to hurt me. The man I loved had used me. And I didn't know why.

I walked back to the front door and exited quickly. If Matt had kept it a secret from me, it meant that he didn't want me to know. I knew that asking him what was going on wasn't going to result in any real answers either. I was sure he had a lie prepared and ready to go if I ever asked him too many questions. I bit my lip as I walked down the empty streets. It was starting to make sense—well, a bit of it was. I'd always been surprised that Matt had never really tried to touch me. He'd never made love to me, and even his kisses had seemed lackluster at times. I thought it was because he was worried that he wouldn't be able to control himself if we got too passionate. Now I wondered if he had been holding back for another reason. What if Brandon had recently started tracking me like I had been tracking him? What if he realized I was dating Matt and had offered him a large sum of money to not sleep with me and to keep tabs on me? He was trying to dictate my love life even though he had a fiancée and didn't want to be with me himself, other than sexually. Of course he wanted me sexually. We couldn't keep our hands off each other. But that meant nothing special. What was sex, really, at the end of the day?

I didn't want to go right home. I didn't want to involve Meg and worry her. I knew that she was stressed as it was. I mean, who wanted to go from being a lawyer to a bartender?

I decided to slip into a bar to have a drink and think. It would stop me from pulling my hair out and crying.

"Vodka on the rocks, please." I slid onto a barstool and smiled at the bartender. He was cute, with an 'I just arrived in the big city' look.

"No chaser?" He smiled.

"Do I look like I need a chaser?" I shook my head and ran my hands through my hair.

"Long day?"

"More like a long seven years." I sighed.

"Want to talk about it?" He gave me a slow, wide smile and I shook my head.

"You don't have all night."

"I could have all night, if you wanted me to." He stared back at me and looked me up and down. I realized that he was flirting with me, and a rush of warmness fled to my skin. I smiled back at him—a lazy, not-interested-but-thank-you smile—and he leaned forward and grabbed my hands. "Don't decide yet. The night is still young." He handed me a glass and I sipped at the vodka. It went smoothly down my throat, warming me up from the inside, and I started to feel a little more relaxed.

"Sex is about power for men. Why is that?" I spoke to the bartender, who had stopped in front of me.

"I don't know. Because women let it be about that?" He shrugged. "So you're mad about a guy? Let me guess, you and your long-term boyfriend recently broke up because you caught him cheating?"

I laughed as he stared at me, looking so confident and sure of himself. He had an arrogant yet sincere vibe about him. I stared at his face clinically. On second glance, he was a lot more handsome than I had first realized.

"So am I right?"

"Does it matter?" I handed him my glass. "Another vodka on the rocks, please. Make it a double."

"Drinking away your sorrows?"

"More like drinking away the questions in my head."

"Why don't you do what we guys do? Just fuck someone else. It's the quickest and easiest way to get over someone."

"I wish it was that easy." I stared at the counter. I hadn't had sex with anyone other than Brandon. I didn't even know what it would feel like to be with another man. I guess I knew why Matt hadn't been interested now. Though I wish I knew the full story.

Beep beep.

I picked up my cell phone and saw a text message from Brandon. I glared at the phone and put it back in my pocket without reading the message. I didn't care what he wanted. I grabbed the new glass that the bartender handed me and downed the vodka in two gulps. I pulled my phone out of my pocket and read the message. I couldn't resist checking it.

"Call me. Now."

I stared at the message for a few minutes before deleting it and putting my phone into my pocket. Who did he think he was? Call him now? Why? Had Maria stepped out to go the gym or something? I was done with being used and abused by him. I was not his plaything.

"Another double, please." I smiled at the bartender and played with my hair.

"Do you want to wait a bit?" He frowned as he looked at me. "You're too pretty to get drunk and make bad mistakes tonight."

"What if you're the bad mistake?" I flirted with him and he paused as he stared at me. He shook his head and poured some more vodka into a new glass.

"Here." He handed me the glass and his fingers grabbed mine. "But this is the last one. If we go home together, I want to know it's because you wanted to be with me and not because you're drunk."

"You're pretty full of yourself." I raised an eyebrow at him, leaned forward, and slowly licked my lips. "If I want another drink, I expect another drink."

"And if you want to fuck me tonight, you need to slow down," he whispered against my lips lightly and his tongue licked my lower lip slowly. I sat back and looked at him in a daze.

"You kissed me." I stared at him in shock, rubbing my fingers against my lips.

"That wasn't a kiss." He winked at me.

"Your lips touched mine."

"Come here." He leaned toward me and I stared up into his bright green eyes in wonder. He bent down and grabbed the back of my head, and his lips pressed against mine firmly as he kissed me properly this time. I felt his tongue trying to work its way into my mouth, but even though I enjoyed the kiss, I wasn't ready to make it more intimate. I pulled away from him, dazed. "Now that was a kiss." He grinned and walked to the other side of the bar to help another customer.

Beep beep.

My phone vibrated and buzzed again. I grabbed it from my pocket and checked my messages. It was Brandon again.

"Katie, you need to call me now."

"Whatever," I mumbled under my breath. "So you can fuck me and leave again?" I was about to put my phone back in my pocket but decided to text back instead. *"Fuck off."* I pressed send.

Within seconds he had replied. *"I can't without you."* I stared at the words, confused.

"That makes no sense," I texted back quickly, wanting to stop responding, but not knowing how.

He texted back immediately again, and for a second, my heart soared that he was thinking of me. *"Call me, Katie. I want to hear your voice."* I stared at his words and wanted to throw the phone to the ground and stomp on it, and then I wanted to stomp on myself. Why was I so happy at his words? Why did I feel like I was flying just because he had texted me a bunch of crap? I wanted to delete his messages and him from my life. I rubbed my lips again, thinking about what the bartender had said. Maybe I did need to have sex with someone else. Maybe that would be the easiest way to get over Brandon. I didn't want him to have this hold over me anymore.

Beep beep.

The phone vibrated again and I stared at the latest message. *"Are you there? Call me, now."* I stared at the phone, feeling tired. My brain was overwhelmed by everything that had happened in the last couple of weeks. And then the phone started ringing. I answered it without thinking.

"Hello?"

"I told you to call me." Brandon's voice was angry.

"So?"

"I want to see you."

"I don't want to see you." I glared into the phone. "What's the *problem*?" I hissed.

"What?"

"Nothing," I mumbled. I didn't want him to know that I knew that he knew Matt. Not yet. Not until I decided what I was going to do.

"I miss you, Katie."

"Where's Maria?"

"Does it matter?"

"What do you think?" My voice rose. "You're an asshole."

"I don't love Maria." His words were firm.

"Piss off!" I shouted into the phone, though my heart leaped with joy at his words. My brain screamed at me to stop feeling excited.

"I want to hold you," he drawled. "I've missed hearing your voice."

"I've got to go," I mumbled, not really wanting to hang up.

"Don't go. Not yet." His voice was urgent. "Where are you? Let me come and take you home."

"How do you know I'm not home?"

"Where are you, Katie?" His voice was harsh.

"What do you care?" I went to have another gulp of vodka, but it was all gone. "Hey, bartender, come here," I called out. He walked over to me slowly with a wicked grin on his face.

"How can I help you, beautiful? Want another kiss?" He laughed and I shook my head.

"Another vodka, please. We can talk about the kiss later." I giggled at him, wanting Brandon to hear the conversation.

"Where the fuck are you, Katie?" Brandon's voice was angrier than I had ever heard before.

"Sorry, I have to go now. Tell Maria I said hello." And then I hung up and turned the phone off so that I wouldn't have to hear it beeping or ringing anymore.

"Who was that?" The bartender handed me a new glass, and I sipped eagerly.

"This tastes like water," I groaned, annoyed and ignoring his question.

"That's because it is." He stared at me. "I don't get involved with girls who have issues or relationship problems, but I'm going to make an exception for you. The only thing is, I don't want you to be passed out when we hook up."

"That's assuming a lot."

"You want to get over your ex, right?" He shrugged. "Trust me, when I'm done with you, you won't even remember his name."

I sat back, sipped the water, and tried to stop the rush of tears that came to my eyes. I couldn't look at the bartender. It didn't matter how hot he was. I couldn't sleep with him, not when all I wanted was Brandon. The bartender stood in front of me, licking his lips sensually, and I jumped off of the barstool and ran out of the bar, not even remembering to pay. I ran down the street, crying and thinking about what the bartender had said so casually. He'd said that by the time he was finished with me, I wouldn't even remember Brandon's name, and my heart broke. I didn't even want to think of a possibility where I couldn't remember Brandon. I loved him with all my heart. And even though my heart was breaking, I didn't want to move on with some casual sex. Not yet. Not now. Not when every part of me was crying out to be with the man I loved. The man I had spent the last seven years thinking about. I loved him as much as I hated him, and I wanted to make him pay. But I needed to do it on my terms. And I needed to plan it out. That was the only way I could be sure that I could finally move on.

I sat on a bench in Central Park for about two hours before some policemen moved me on. I saw the concern in their eyes as they looked at my tear-streaked face, but they didn't ask me what was wrong. I suppose they knew better than to ask a crying lady what was wrong unless she was walking up to them with an issue. I was tired when I finally got to my apartment complex. I was standing at the main door, searching for my keys when I felt someone grab me. I tried to scream, but my voice was hoarse and nothing came out.

"Where have you been?" Brandon's nostrils flared as he stared down at me with darkened eyes.

"Out." I pulled away from him, my heart beating faster.

"With the bartender." His voice was angry and he held me tight. "Did you fuck him?"

"It's none of your business." I glared up at him and tried to push him away.

"Tell me." His voice was hoarse and his eyes looked into mine, searching for an answer. "Did you fuck him?"

"What do you care?"

"Does your boyfriend know you're tramping it around the city?"

"How dare you!" I found a sudden burst of energy and pushed him off of me. "Just leave me alone, jackass."

"Where have you been? I've been waiting for you to come home for the last two hours."

I turned my face away from him, not wanting to answer.

"Your phone isn't on." He pulled me towards him again. "I've been calling and calling. I thought something happened."

"As you can see, I'm fine." I rolled my eyes.

"Act your age, Katie," he hissed, angry again. "You're not eighteen anymore."

"And you're not my boyfriend anymore." I stared at him and laughed bitterly. "You may think you can have me when you want me, but those days are gone. I'm not going to sleep with you again."

"Is that so?" His eyes glittered like diamonds in the dark.

"Yes." My hands crept to his chest to push him away again, but instead they caressed his pecs. "You're never going to have this"—I pointed to myself—"again."

"But what if I want it again?" He tilted his head and stared at my breasts. "What if I want you tonight?"

"I don't think you want sloppy seconds," I shot back at him. He drew his breath in sharply.

"I know you didn't sleep with that man." He pushed me back against the doorway and I gasped.

"How?" I squeaked out with eyes wide open.

"Because," he said as he leaned towards me and pressed his lips against mine, "you're mine." His hand slid up my shirt and cupped my right breast. "Your body is mine. I possess you and only I can have you." His lips crushed down on mine and my legs buckled slightly as my body convulsed with pleasure underneath him.

"I'm not yours." I shook my head as my hands ran up his back. "You have a fiancée," I whispered against his lips. "You have a son."

"You're still mine," he growled against my lips. "I told you that night in Doug's, if you continued on that night, if we made love, I would possess you. I'm never going to let you go."

"I'm quitting," I whispered before his tongue entered my mouth. I was too weak to say no. I held on to his shoulders as his tongue explored every inch of my mouth. He pushed himself into me and I felt his erection against my lower belly. His fingers squeezed my nipple and his lips were dominating mine in their quest.

"You're not going anywhere." He leaned back and stared into my still stunned eyes.

"You can't stop me." I shivered as his fingers switched to my other breast. A man walked past us in the street and I could see him staring at us and mumbling something to himself. I was half surprised that he hadn't stopped to watch the show. "I have to go inside now."

"I'm coming up."

"No." I shook my head. "No, you can't."

"I want to see your apartment." He smiled then. "I've never seen any of your apartments."

145

I stared at him then as I realized that he was correct. "How did you know where I live?" I frowned as it dawned on me that I had never given him my address.

"There's nothing about you that I don't know, Katie." His eyes pierced into mine. "Now let me in, or I'll make love to you in the street."

"You'd like that, wouldn't you?" I glared at him. "Why don't you just bend me over the dumpster again and leave?"

"I made a mistake," he sighed. "I shouldn't have done that."

"Well, you did."

"Are you ever going to forgive me for that?"

"I already forgave you," I said softly, and his eyes looked at me in hope. I felt weird as he stared at me. It almost felt like he still cared, but he'd fooled me once before. "I forgave you for that, but I don't forgive you for fucking me while you have a fiancée."

"Did you enjoy his kiss?"

"What?" I stared at him, confused. "What are you talking about? I'm talking about you having sex with me while you have a fiancée."

"Did you enjoy it when the guy in the bar kissed you?" His body looked stiff and his expression was frozen.

"Why are you asking me this?"

"No reason." He shook his head and sighed. "I should go."

"Don't let me stop you."

"Let me see you upstairs to your apartment first."

"No."

"Katie."

"Fine." I sighed, not wanting to be away from him just yet anyway. I opened the front door and we walked up the stairs slowly until we got to the third floor. "Okay, see ya." I stopped outside a door and he laughed.

"I know you live on the fifth floor, Katie. I also know there is an elevator in this building."

146

"How'd you know that?" I asked grumpily.

"I own the building."

"Oh." I frowned and my mind started churning again. "Since when?"

"Does it matter?"

"I guess not." I shrugged. "Fine, come on." I started up the steps again and then stopped, feeling out of breath and tired.

"I take it you don't walk up the stairs much?" He grinned.

"I'm just tired," I said, panting.

"You need to work out more." He laughed at me as I bent over, trying to catch my breath.

"Are you calling me fat?" I asked him indignantly.

"No." He grabbed me and picked me up.

"What are you doing?" I struggled against him.

"I'm carrying you up, of course." He walked up the stairs easily with me in his arms. When we got to the fifth floor, he walked directly to my apartment and then put me down. "Open the door," he ordered me.

"Yes, sir," I muttered back to him.

"I like it when you call me sir." He grinned.

"Don't get used to it," I shot back.

"Trust me, I know." He followed me into the apartment. "You like to be on top too much to be a submissive."

"Shut up!" I gasped and hit him in the arm. "You can leave now."

"I don't want to leave." He shook his head.

"Shh." I made a big deal of telling him to be quiet. "Meg is probably sleeping. I don't want to wake her."

"Then let's go to your room."

"Sorry, but I have someone coming over." I stared at him. "He won't appreciate you being here with me."

"Who's coming over? Matt?"

"No, the guy in the bar. He was a bartender. He's coming here after work. So I need to go shower and get ready for him now."

"Are you trying to bait me, Katie?" His voice was low as he took a step toward me.

"No." I shook my head and took a step back.

"What's his name?"

"Whose name?" I blinked at him, trying to think fast.

"The bartender."

"I didn't ask him his name." I swallowed hard. "We kissed and then fucked and then I left to get the apartment ready."

"You didn't fuck him." Brandon shook his head, looking furious.

"Maybe not, but I thought about it." I stared at him straight on. "As he kissed me, I thought about fucking him hard. I almost came just thinking about it."

"I'll make you pay for that." His voice was low as he grabbed my arms and pulled me toward him.

"What are you doing?" My breathing was hard and my body was trembling in sweet anticipation.

"I'm going to make you wish you had never met that bartender."

"He tasted like cotton candy and gin," I whispered against his lips. His eyes darkened as he gaze turned murderous. His lips crashed down on mine hard, his teeth biting my lower lip aggressively as his tongue plunged into my mouth. His kiss was all-consuming and devastating. This wasn't a sweet kiss of love; this was a kiss of passion and domination. I melted into his arms as he made me his once again. My every nerve ending responded to his colonization, and I whimpered when he pulled away from me slowly, running his hands through his hair as he stared at my lips.

"You're bleeding."

"It doesn't hurt." I licked my lips and tasted a faint drop of blood. "It's nothing." He bent down again, and this time his tongue licked my lips softly before he sucked on my lower lip. "What are you doing?"

"Licking the blood away."

"Are you a vampire?" I joked and he laughed as he pulled me toward him and kissed my forehead.

"When I'm with you, I feel like I could be one."

"What does that mean?"

"Nothing." He shook his head. "Let me see your room."

"No."

"That's not go through this again." He grabbed my hand. "Take me to your room."

"I can't."

"Stop with the games. We both know no one is coming tonight. I'm already mad enough that you kissed someone else."

"Whatever." I tried to pull away from him as my insides grew warm with desire.

"Katie." He pulled me toward him again and looked down at me seriously. "Don't push me."

I wanted to whisper, "Or what?" but no words would come out. He squeezed my hand and led me to my bedroom door. I frowned as he walked in and locked it behind us. He pushed me down on the bed and then lay down next to me. His hand ran up my stomach and to my breast, and he gazed at me with lust in his eyes.

"I'm going to make sweet love to you, Katie. Like you want me to."

I stared at him, unable to deny that I wanted him.

"Don't kiss anyone else." His voice sounded strangely bleak.

"I can kiss who I want." My heart started pounding.

"I'll leave Maria." His words were soft, but they grinded my heart to a stop.

"What?"

"I'll break the engagement off with Maria." He held my hands. "If that will stop you from being with other men."

"What about Harry?"

"Let me worry about him." He averted his gaze from

mine.

"I don't understand." I looked back at him. "Do you still love me?" I was hopeful as I stared at him in front of me, all broody and dark. I felt like I was at the edge of a cliff about to jump into the water and only he could stop me from jumping.

"I never stopped loving you, Katie." The words made my heart jump, but his expression was still dark and tormented. "It's never been about me loving you."

"Then what's it been about?" All color left my face as I stared at him.

"It's been about you and if you're ready. If you've finally grown up. If you see love as a real and deep emotion that can't be toyed with or if this all still a game to you." His words sounded angry.

"I see." I swallowed hard, upset inside. His words had hurt me. I couldn't believe that once again he was harping on about my age. Was I never going to be able to move on from that one small lie?

"Your skin is so soft. It reminds me of rose petals." His fingers trailed down my cheek and his lips nibbled on my ear.

"Why are you changing the subject again?" I breathed out, running my hands through his hair.

"What do you want to talk about?" he whispered in my ear.

"Are we getting back together?" I whispered back, turning my lips to his.

"Let's talk about this later." His lips came down on mine and I closed my eyes as I melted into him. My brain was happy and my heart was dancing. Brandon was going to leave Maria, and that was all I cared about. Maybe we really did have a shot at a future together. And then I felt my insides freeze. There was still the issue with Matt. How did he know Matt? How could I be sure he wasn't playing me again?

"Let me be on top." I pushed him down on the bed,

slowly unbuckled his belt, and pulled his pants down. His cock struggled against his white boxer briefs and I groaned as he pulled me down on top of him.

"See how hard I am for you?" he growled against my ear as he pulled my top off. He unclasped my bra and threw it on the floor before pushing me up slightly and taking my left breast in his mouth. My body shuddered as his hands slid down my back and squeezed my ass. His fingers quickly undid my pants and I wiggled on top of him as he pulled them down my legs. I pulled his boxer briefs off slowly as I kissed down his stomach, and I smiled to myself when his body stilled as my mouth neared his hardness. I kissed down his shaft softly, enjoying the feeling of power I had over him in this moment. I could make him cry out my name and beg me to satisfy him if I wanted to. I took him into my mouth and he groaned as I sucked on him wholly. I loved the salty, raw taste of him. He was all man and I was all woman, and I held his fate in my mouth. I took him deep into my mouth, wanting to taste every inch of him. His cock jittered in my mouth and he looked up at me with a hooded gaze.

"Katie," he groaned as I slowly pulled back and sucked on his tip, licking the pre-cum off of the tip before sitting up and sliding my body onto him. I positioned the head of his cock between my legs and allowed the tip to gently rub my clit as I moved back and forth, pleasuring myself with him. "Katie," he groaned louder this time. "Please."

I smiled down at him, almost forgetting that I hated him as much as I loved him. All I could think of was Matt's call. What problem did they have? I needed to know how Brandon knew Matt. I reached down and caressed his cock again before slowly sliding down on it. I moaned as he filled me up and my juices covered his hardness. I sat on top of him and rode him slowly, allowing his cock to slide in and out of me before twirling my hips. He groaned as I increased my pace, and I watched as he closed his eyes. I looked down at him as I fucked him, and I knew that this was my opportunity to get some answers. I increased my pace even more, and his hands reached up to grab my breasts as I rode him. And then I slowed my pace until I completely stopped moving.

He opened his eyes slowly and groaned. "Don't stop, Katie."

"I want to ask you a question," I said softly and moved back and forth slowly. I could feel his cock twitching inside of me.

"What?" he groaned as his hands moved to my hips to try and force my movements to go faster.

"I want to know how you know my ex-boyfriend, Matt?" I sat up until his cock was completely out of me and then sat back down and started grinding on him but not allowing him to enter me.

"Katie." His eyes darkened as he tried to adjust his cock to be inside of me.

"Tell me." I reached down, grabbed his cock, and let the tip of him enter me. "How do you know Matt?" I thought I had won as he groaned and sat up slightly, but then Brandon grabbed ahold of me until I was flat on my stomach. I felt him lower his body onto mine before slipping his cock back inside of me. He moved quickly, and I closed my eyes as pleasure overtook everything in my mind. I gasped as I felt him going deeper and deeper. He then pulled out quickly and flipped me onto my back before entering me again.

"I want to see your face when you come for me." He grinned down at me as he increased his pace.

"Tell me," I gasped. "How do you know Matt?"

Brandon was quiet for a moment as he fucked me. I could feel his orgasm building up, and my body started shuddering as his fingers played with me as he fucked me. I closed my eyes as my orgasm built up, and he slammed into me a few more times before I felt him burst inside of me. I climaxed a few seconds after him and clung to him as our bodies shook together.

"His dad works for me," he whispered in my ear. "Matt is Maria's brother."

CHAPTER 2
BRANDON

Matt's phone call had stopped my heart. I hadn't waited all these years and come this far for Katie to just give up on me. I couldn't let it happen. I wasn't going to let it happen. All my life I had gone from woman to woman, not knowing what love was and not caring, and then I met Katie. Katie of my heart and soul. Katie who set my heart on fire with one smile. The moment I saw her, I knew she was the one. Something about the way her eyes stared into mine with her shy smile, the way her hair always curled no matter how much she straightened it. There was something about her that couldn't be tamed. Yet, she appealed to me. She was the love of my life. But now, she was giving up on me.

I watched as Harry played with his Legos, carefully pushing the pieces on top of each other. I loved him more than life itself. My son, the flesh of my loins. I'd never experienced a love like this before. He was the symbol of all my dreams come true, and I would not let him experience the pain I'd had to experience. Before I made any changes in our lives, I had to be one hundred percent sure that he wasn't going to get hurt. That was why I'd left Katie early this morning. I knew she would be upset that I had left while she was asleep, but as I'd lain with her, watching her sleep, I'd known that I was too weak. I hadn't wanted to leave. I hadn't wanted to let her go again. It was becoming increasingly hard to not say to hell with everything and just stay with her. But there was too much at stake. There was Harry to think of now. And I knew that, to a lesser extent, I had to take Maria into account. And my promise to Will. And I couldn't forget what had happened with Denise. I closed my eyes as I thought about Denise—she was the reason for all of this. If I could only turn back time—then I wouldn't be in this mess.

Last night had been hard. When Matt called me, I knew that I didn't have much time left. I couldn't let her leave Marathon Corporation. I knew that if she left, everything would have been for naught. I was mad at myself when I got off the phone with Matt. I had pushed Katie too far and too fast, and she was already breaking. And now she had kissed another man. I wanted to hit someone at the thought. I grew angry and jealous at the thought of her making love to another man. She hadn't last night, but who knows what stopped her. I was sure that it hadn't been for the lack of the bartender trying. I was going to have to find out what bar she had gone to and have a *talk* with the bartender, just in case Katie went in there again and had any ideas. My insides felt like they were going to burst out of my stomach. I clenched my fists as I thought about her kissing another man and enjoying it. I had done everything in my power to get us to this moment, and it wasn't working out as planned. Not at all.

I thought back to the first night I met her. It was the best and worst night of my life.

The first time I saw her was at 1:30 a.m. I could still remember it as clear as day. I had been walking home when I saw her standing there, looking so lost and innocent. She had been standing against the wall and dancing and singing to herself with a huge smile on her face. I hadn't been able to stop myself from going up to her, even though I hadn't wanted to. My insides had screamed at me to move on, but there was something about her that had made me grind to a halt.

"Are you okay?" Outside the trashy club, I'd approached her apprehensively, hoping not to scare her.

As I got closer to her, I realized that her face looked pale. I immediately felt concerned for her, though my brain was screaming at me to leave her alone. I knew that Doug's was a bar full of miscreants, and after the last couple of weeks I'd had, I wasn't interested in meeting any new women.

"Do you need me to take you somewhere?" The words were out of my mouth before I could stop them, and my hands gripped her shoulders. As soon as I touched her, I felt a buzz of electricity run through me. She looked up at me then, her big brown eyes friendly and surprised. She studied my face for a few seconds before grinning at me in appreciation.

"I'm fine." She giggled slightly and moved closer to me. A part of me wanted to kiss her right then and there. She captivated me with her openness. It was something I wasn't used to. "I'm just waiting on my friends." Her words slurred and she hiccupped.

I looked around the street to see if I could see any other girls. There was no one else outside, aside from one of the bouncers and a seedy looking man who was staring at her legs. I glared at him before turning back to her angrily. What was she doing standing outside this sleazy club by herself? Didn't she know what could happen?

"You're drunk. I'm not seeing any friends here."

"They're in the ladies' room." She stumbled towards me.

"I see. I'll wait with you then." I took her hand and we leaned against the wall, waiting for her friends to come out. She stared at me again with a sweet smile.

"Thank you," she said softly and I nodded at her, not

knowing what to say.

This girl was different, with her big, wavy hair and cheap, overdone makeup. She didn't fit the sleek, made-up look of other women in the city. A part of me was attracted to her for all she represented, and the other part of me was attracted to her because she was sexy as hell.

"Are you trying to seduce me?" She wiggled her eyebrows at me while staring at me with obvious lust as she giggled and pushed her chest out. I appreciated the fact that she was showing me who she was and what she wanted, even though I knew there was no way I would sleep with her now. Not when she was drunk. Not after what had happened with Denise. I'd be a fool to go down that road. I declined her offer and smiled at her. There was something so lost but genuine about her. Standing there brought out feelings I had never felt before. This girl was different, and I was loath to just leave her alone.

I can still remember my brain screaming at me as I offered to take her home with me that night. I suppose I could have asked to see her driver's license and sent her off in a cab, but I wanted to make sure she was okay. And I wanted a chance to see what she was like when she wasn't drunk. I helped her back to my apartment slowly. I was mad at the fact that she went with me so easily. She fell asleep and became dead weight in my arms about two blocks from my apartment, so I picked her up and carried her back quickly, feeling like her knight in shining armor. Only, she didn't know, and I knew that there was no one else who would ever call me a Prince Charming. I'd placed her in the bed and gone to sleep on the couch in the living room. I didn't want her to wake up in bed with a strange man and panic, even though I'd wanted to feel her in my arms.

The next morning she woke up with a trusting face and a huge but weary smile, and I knew she wasn't like all the others. She was different, and as she looked at me so guilelessly, I knew that I wanted a relationship with her.

But I couldn't forget what had just happened with Denise, so I called Will and asked him to check her out and follow her. I just needed to know that she wasn't setting me up. It was the second-worst decision of my life, and once again, now I felt like everything was crashing down around me.

"Ow," Harry whimpered, and I was immediately brought back to the present.

"What's wrong?" I hurried over to him.

"My Lego hurt me." He grinned at me and jumped up. "I want to go and play on my new skateboard now."

"Not right now, Harry." I shook my head and ruffled his hair.

"Oh come on, Dad. I'll be careful." He looked up at me with a hopeful expression and a small pout. He reminded me so much of his mother with his expressive face. I hugged him to me for a second and shook my head. "Maybe tomorrow."

"You always say that." He frowned and pulled away from me. "I'm going to go and play Wii."

"Maybe I'll join you in a few minutes," I called after him as he ran out of the room, and he looked back at me with such a look of joy that I told myself I definitely needed to play with him after my call.

"Hello?" Matt answered slowly and unsurely. I knew he was worried about my tone. I had been furious with him last night.

"Matt, it's Brandon."

"She's not answering my calls, sir."

"That's fine." I bit my lower lip, not sure how to continue. "Right now I need you to focus on something else."

"Sure. Do you want me to look into another company?" His voice grew excited at the possibility, and I sighed internally. He wasn't as good a detective as his father Will had been. I knew his heart wasn't in the job, not if it wasn't to do with business. Matt was a journalist first and foremost, a detective second. And I didn't trust him, not like I had trusted his dad. But when his dad died of a heart attack two years ago, he had taken over the business, and I'd remained loyal to honor his dad.

"No, I need you to find a bar."

"A bar?" His tone sounded surprised.

"I need to know the name of the bar Katie went to last night when she left your apartment. And I need to know the names of all the bartenders that were working last night."

"How am I supposed to find that out?" Matt sounded bored, and I wanted to reach through the phone and smack him. Matt irritated me, and if it weren't for all he'd done so far and all the information he knew, I would have told him what I thought of him. The only reason I'd hired Matt to date Katie was because I knew he was gay. No matter what happened, he was never going to seduce her and have sex with her. And I didn't care about a few sloppy kisses—not from him. I knew he could never set her on fire like I did.

"Do some work." My tone was angry. "Go through her credit card bills, see who saw her in the street, check every neighborhood bar around you with photos, do whatever it takes. But get me that information."

"Sure," he sighed.

"I want it by tonight."

"But I was planning on—" He started and I coldly interrupted him.

"I don't care what your plans were. I need this information by tonight."

"You only care about yourself," he muttered with a bitter tone.

"Don't forget who got you the job at the *Wall Street Journal*," I hissed. "And don't forget who's looking after your sister."

"How is Maria, by the way?" His voice was glib. "Should I reserve a date on my calendar for the wedding?"

"Funny." My tone was anything but humorous.

160

"I dare say she wouldn't mind being a part of some sort of sister wives marriage," he joked. "Seeing as you like the group stuff anyways."

My blood boiled over at his comment. I knew that he was sending me a warning, not just idly joking. But he had no idea who he was messing with.

"Matt, just get me the information." I hung up the phone and rubbed my temples. That was the problem with having too many people in your business. Will had been the only other person who knew what had gone down with Denise and me that night. And now it seemed that Matt knew as well. I knew then and there that it was over for him as well as for Maria. I'd done as much as I could to help them and honor their father's wishes, but I could take them no further. I didn't care how cruel I had to be.

I called Katie's number and waited with bated breath to see if she was going to answer.

"Hello?" Her voice was standoffish, but she answered after one ring.

"Sorry I had to leave early this morning."

"You did?" Her voice faked surprise. "I didn't even notice you weren't here when I woke up."

"I didn't want to leave." I wished my words could convey the depth of my feelings for her.

"Whatever. You hit it and quit it. That's your usual M.O." Her voice sounded harsh.

"Katie." I was getting angry. "That's not what happened."

"What do you want, Brandon?" she sighed.

"To talk," I said softly, though I really wanted to say, "You. I want you."

"Well, talk then." She sounded irritated. "I have to go."

"Don't quit."

"Maybe you shouldn't have hired your fiancée's brother to date me." She was angry. "And what exactly does his dad do for you?"

"I don't want to talk about it. I told you. Not now." I

gripped the phone. I hadn't been completely honest with Katie when she had asked how I knew Matt. I'd been in shock when she asked me, on the point of orgasm, and my brain wasn't able to comprehend the depth of how scared I had been. If she'd stayed around to hear more of Matt's conversation with me, she would have figured out that he was now working for me instead of his dad. There was silence on the phone and my heart dropped. "Katie." I talked into the phone, but I knew she had hung up on me.

I called her back, but this time she didn't answer. I wanted to throw the phone into the wall when I heard the call go to voicemail. I was so angry and worried. What if I had lost her? After everything that had happened, I knew there was a high possibility that she was done with me. And what did I expect? I was forty-two, and she was twenty-five. I'd always wanted to give her space so she could make her own decisions. I'd always known it was a risk and that things might not work out as I hoped. But it had been seven years. I'd sacrificed everything for this moment and opportunity, and it looked like my worst fears were coming true.

"Dad, you coming?" Harry shouted from the living room, and I put my phone in my pocket. I'd try calling Katie again later. Now I needed to be with my son.

***

"I was thinking we should set a date." Maria walked into my study with a tight smile. She had asked me to talk while Harry and I were playing Mario Kart, and I'd told her to come and see me later. Now I wished that I hadn't.

"A date?" I looked up at her blankly.

"For the wedding." She walked behind the desk and sat on my lap. "Silly."

"What are you talking about?" I sat back, uncomfortable with the way she was moving against me.

"I'm ready to get married and make this real." She

leaned in toward me and I jumped up.

"This isn't real, Maria." I shook my head as I felt my heart pounding.

"It wasn't at first, but now it is." She stood up and grabbed my shirt. "I know at first you only started dating me as a favor to my dad, but we're in love now."

"Maria, we never dated." I tried to keep my voice gentle, as I knew how fragile she was. "And we aren't in love."

"I love you, Brandon." Her eyes looked upset. "We're a family."

"We're not a family, Maria." I shook my head, fear forming in my stomach.

"I spoke to Matt last night." Her voice changed. "I know that Katie's done with you. She's quitting and wants nothing to do with you. It's time to move on now, Brandon," she pleaded with me and her fingers ran down my arm. "It's time to give that dream up."

"That's none of your business, Maria." My voice was hard.

"I'll tell her the truth if you don't marry me." Maria looked up at me with ice in her blue eyes. "I will tell her the truth and that would ruin everything."

"You don't know what you're talking about." I called her bluff.

"My dad told me everything that he did for you." Her fingers ran down the front of my pants, but my cock remained frozen and still. "I know everything." She tilted her head and looked up at me. "What time of year would you like the wedding to take place?"

"Your father would be ashamed of you if he knew what you were doing." I grabbed ahold of her wrist and pulled her hand away from me. "You're disgracing the family name."

"What do I care?" She looked at me with anger in her eyes. "They didn't care about me when they pawned me off to you."

"I've tried to help you."

"Because you love me." Her voice softened and her eyes looked at me adoringly. "You've taken me in because you love me." She rested her head against my chest and I stood there, immobile. I hadn't counted on Maria trying to make this difficult. I decided to save my breakup talk for the next day; I couldn't afford for Maria to go rogue on me—not now. Not when everything was still so precarious with Katie. If Maria really knew everything, then I was in big trouble. She would have the power to topple my deck of cards and have everything come crumbling down around me.

"I have to go out." I extricated myself from her embrace and quickly left the study. Maria was going to make this difficult—very difficult indeed.

"Wait." She grabbed my arm. "Kiss me before you go."

"Maria," My voice was stern as I pulled away from her. "Go and get your bags packed."

"Why?"

"I think it's time for you to move." I cleared my throat. "It's been nice having you here, but it is time for you to move on."

"You told my father you would look after me."

"I've given you a roof over your head. I've protected you as best as I can, but enough is enough."

"It's because of that whore, isn't it? Maria spat out with hatred in her eyes.

"It's time for you to go." I turned around and walked out of the room before I did or said something I would regret.

"You'll never have her, you know!" Maria called out. "Not by the time I'm done. You two will never have a relationship. Not when she knows the truth."

"Maria, I'm warning you." I took a step away from her, hatred burning in me.

"I know about the whores, you know." Her eyes danced with evil joy as she studied me. "And I know about

164

the files. I wonder if innocent little Katie knows. There's quite a lot she doesn't know, isn't there?" She grabbed my hand and placed it on her breast. "Just make love to me, Brandon. Just make love to me so we can make a brother or sister for Harry. Then I won't tell. I won't tell Katie."

"Don't threaten me." My voice was cold and deadly as I pulled my hand away. "You do not want to mess with me, Maria."

"I think it's you that shouldn't mess with me, dear Brandon." She smiled and took a step back. "Where's Harry? I want to go and read him a story."

"He's gone to my dad's house." I felt myself thanking God for getting my dad and his new girlfriend to pick up Harry for the rest of the week. I'd had a feeling that shit was going to hit the fan, and I knew Maria would try to involve him.

"You didn't ask me." She glared at me.

"I didn't need to ask you."

"He's my son!" she screamed, her eyes blazing.

"No, Maria." I shook my head and looked into her eyes. "He's never been your son."

"She's never going to take you back, you know." Her eyes looked at me with a bitter glee. "Not once she knows everything."

I turned away from her abruptly and left the house. I didn't hit women, but I had come mighty close to slapping her. But I wasn't even mad at Maria; I was mad at myself.

About thirty minutes later, I found myself outside of Katie's apartment. I needed to see her. I needed to feel her. I called her phone and waited for her to answer.

"Hello?"

"You answered."

"What do you want, Brandon?"

"Can I see you?"

"No."

"Can I come over?"

"No." Her voice was firm. "I'm having an early night.

I'm going to bed now."

"I can be there within five minutes."

"Sorry. No." And then she hung up on me again.

I stood there outside her front door, wanting to just open it up and go inside. No one told me no. But I didn't. I knew I couldn't invade her privacy like that. What if she moved out? I couldn't risk losing every connection I had with her. I started walking down the stairs when the phone rang. I grabbed it eagerly, thinking it was Katie.

"You changed your mind?"

"Mr. Hastings?" Matt's voice sounded surprised.

"What is it, Matt?"

"I found the bar." He sounded proud of himself.

"I see. How do you know?"

"There are only three bars near me." His voice sounded obnoxious.

"That doesn't answer my question." My voice grew angry as I became frustrated. "How do you know which one she went to?"

"Well, I happened to be in there just now." His voice was quick and excited. "I was sitting in a corner booth. It's dark in the corners so people can't really see you, but you can see them."

"Get on with it," I growled.

"Well, I was sitting there, and Katie just walked in." My heart stopped at his words and I hit the wall as I exited the building.

"And?"

"And the bartender looked up at her and smiled." Matt's voice rose. "And he said, 'Well, this must be my lucky week! I get to see your pretty face two days in a row.'"

"I see."

"So obviously, she must have been there last night," Matt continued. "And I think something happened. Because when she sat down, he offered everyone at the bar blowjob shots. He said that everyone deserved to get as lucky as he was going to get tonight."

"What's the name of the bar?" I growled, furious.

"Getting Lucky," Matt drawled. "I just left the bar and Katie was there flirting with the bartender. He also owns the place. But yeah, the name is Getting Lucky. And I guess we both know what's going to go down tonight."

I hung up, and this time I did throw my phone against the wall. I watched as it cracked and fell to the ground. Katie had blown me off and lied to me. I wasn't happy, and there was no way in hell I was going to let some chump come in and steal my woman away from me. Not after everything I'd been through. Even if I had to play rough and dirty, I was going to make sure that there wasn't ever going to be a relationship between Katie and the bartender.

CHAPTER 3
KATIE

"I don't know if I should take the job." Meg made a face. "Not that I've gotten the job yet. I guess the first interview was just a screening interview."

"A job's a job, right?" I yawned from the couch, my mind elsewhere.

"I'm just not sure if everything is as it seems, you know?"

"What do you mean?" I frowned and looked up at her.

"I don't really know if it's a regular bar. The girl who interviewed me said it was a private club."

"A private club?"

"Yeah, I don't know more," Meg sighed. "I guess I'll find out next week." She sat next to me. "So what about you? Where've you been?"

"Just had to go out for a bit." I leaned back into the couch. "Brandon was here last night."

"I kinda heard." Meg laughed.

"Oh." I blushed. "Sorry."

"Are you guys back together again?"

"No." I shook my head. "I can't deal with him anymore. I know I've said this many times before, but this time I'm really done."

"It's just all so weird." Meg's eyes grew round. "You get a job at his company and begin a whirlwind sexual adventure with him so quickly."

"Oh, Meg," I giggled. "I don't know that I would say we began any sort of sexual adventure. We had some hot sex a few times and I felt like a fool."

"You're not a fool." She shook her head.

"I'm a fool in love." My phone beeped, but I ignored it and turned to her. "There's something you don't know."

"What?"

"When Brandon bought Marathon Corporation, I wasn't in as much shock as you thought."

"What?"

"I kind of knew he was going to buy the company."

"What? How?" Her voice rose.

"Don't judge me," I groaned and leaned back. "This is going to sound crazy."

"Oh my God, Katie. Tell me."

"So you know how much I loved Brandon, right? How much I thought he was the one."

"Yeah." She nodded.

"Well, I guess I never really got over him. I never forgot about him."

"He was a douche, Katie. For what he did. And for leaving you like that. All the things you had to go through by yourself." Meg's voice was passionate. "I'm sorry, but I kinda hate him."

"He didn't know about everything." I bit my lip as I stared at her.

"What do you mean?" She blinked rapidly.

"I mean, I never spoke to him after that day at school. The day he found out I was eighteen. I was hoping he would contact me, but he never did," I sighed. "So I just did what I had to do."

"Oh my God, Katie." Meg's hand flew to her mouth. "But you told me you told him. You told me that he didn't care and he wanted nothing to do with you because you lied."

"I'm so ashamed of myself, Meg." I stared at the wall to avoid seeing the shock in her eyes. "I never told him. I figured if he loved me he would have contacted me. He would have begged me to come back to him. And so I was young and selfish and immature, and I made a rash decision."

"Oh, Katie. Does he know?"

"How could I tell him, Meg?" I shook my head. "There hasn't really been a chance."

"Oh." Meg grabbed my hands and squeezed. "Don't beat yourself up. We all make mistakes."

"Yeah." I gave her a small smile. "So a few years ago, I started really looking into what he was doing. Reading every article I could find about him. Tracking his business stuff, and I even called his office a few times to hear his voice."

"Wow."

"I know, I know. It was crazy. At one point, I almost thought he knew it was me." I sighed. "But I think it was just wishful thinking. I started following a journalist who had written a lot of pieces on him and went to a party that his newspaper was hosting. I knew his photo from the paper, and when I saw him, I accidentally bumped into him."

"Oh shit, not Matt?" Meg was bug-eyed now.

"Yeah, Matt."

"I knew you didn't like him!" Meg exclaimed.

"What?"

"He just never really looked like your type. I mean, he was nice and all, but he wasn't really exciting, and you guys never really seemed to have chemistry."

"Yeah, well, get this. So I became friendly with him to try and get more information on Brandon, but..."

"Oh my God, but what?" Meg looked at me with excitement on her face. I knew that she was loving every minute of this scandalous conversation.

"Matt"—I paused dramatically—"is working for Brandon."

"WHAT?" Meg screamed as she stared at me in shock. "Brandon Hastings? Are you telling me that Matt, your boyfriend, works for Brandon, your ex?"

"Yup." I nodded. "Crazy, right?"

"What the fuck?" Meg shook her head. "So was Matt working for Brandon when you met him or more recently?"

"No idea." I bit my lower lip. "That's what I want to know as well."

"This is crazy. You played someone, but maybe you were played from the beginning?"

"Yeah," I sighed. "It's so confusing."

"This is like a frigging movie." Meg jumped up. "I need a glass of wine. Want one?"

"Yeah, go on." I sat back in the couch and waited for Meg to come back with the wine.

"Here you go." She handed me a glass and sat back down. "Okay, okay, so let me get this straight. You tried to find Brandon 'cause you still missed him? Why didn't you just go straight to one of his offices or something?"

"I wanted it to be an organic meeting." I rolled my eyes. "Don't ask. At the time, I thought it was a good idea to make it seem like a chance meeting."

"So you bumped into Matt so you could get insider information on Brandon. Which you got. You then got a job at a company you knew he was buying so that you could pretend to be worried when he was back in your life, but really you were excited. You hooked up with him, hoping that meant that he wanted you back, but instead he treated you like shit again and you found out he had a fiancée and a son. Then you slept with him again and he treated you like shit again. And now you want to leave the job and forget any of this ever happened."

"I guess that's why you're the lawyer." I gave her a half smile. "You got it all in one paragraph."

"Well, I'm no longer employed as a lawyer." She made a face. "But this is one hell of a story."

"I know. I feel like a bit of a psycho," I muttered, thinking about everything. "I can't believe I've wasted so much time on this guy and he's just an asshole."

"I agree that he's an asshole, but I think he deserves to know the truth," Meg said softly, and I looked up into her earnest eyes with a frown. "I know it's hard, Katie. And you probably try not to think about it, but I think you need to tell him what happened. Maybe that's part of the reason why you can't move on."

"It hurts too much." I bit my lower lip, desperately trying to forget what I'd done.

Meg leaned over and rubbed my shoulder. "But at least you know. He doesn't even know."

"Yeah, I guess. I just never want to see him again," I groaned.

"Don't lie, Katie." Meg laughed. "You love him. There's nothing wrong with that, but I do agree. It's time to move on. I think he's being an asshole and he's cheating on his fiancée. He's not a nice guy. Yeah, he has a son and seems to love him, but why would he potentially ruin his family by sleeping with you? He's an egomaniac and a jerk. He likes the power of taking whatever woman he feels like taking. He doesn't seem to care about you at all. I mean, why would he be doing all of this?"

"I just don't get it. I know I lied when we dated. I know I hurt him. But he hurt me too." I sighed. "I don't know why he's still trying to hurt me."

"Maybe you need to have an honest conversation with him. Tell him everything and ask him to let you be. You need to move on, Katie. Meet a new guy. A nice guy."

"I kinda met someone." I made a face. "Well, we kissed."

"What? You met someone and didn't tell me?" Meg looked at me, clearly hurt.

"Just recently. And I'm not really interested in him.

He's a bartender at Getting Lucky's. He kinda gave me a kiss and hinted that he'd like to do more."

"Is he hot?"

"He's sexy and hot." I laughed and then sighed. "I just can't think of anyone else that way though."

"Katie, you need to stop letting this guy ruin all your potential relationships. He is not worth it." Meg shook her head. "Have a final conversation with him. End it. And move on."

"Yeah, I guess you're right." I sipped on my wine. "Someone has been texting me all night. Let me see if it's him."

"If it's him, tell me what he said and I will tell you what to text back."

"Argh, okay." I laughed, jumped up, and grabbed my phone. "Okay, here are his texts. First one. 'Hey Katie, I hope you're enjoying your night in. If you want company let me know.'" I laughed. "Sure, Brandon. I'm going to text you right now."

"Read the rest."

"Okay, number two. 'Hey Katie, I sure hope you're not doing anything you're going to regret right now.'"

"What does that mean?" Meg frowned.

"No idea." I shrugged. "Okay, number three. 'Katie, I need you to call me right now.' Number four. 'Katie, text me back or call now.' Number five. 'Katie, stop playing games. Call me now.' Number six. 'Katie, I don't know what the fuck you're doing, but call me now.' What the fuck is his problem?" I groaned, but inside I felt a secret excitement that he wanted to talk to me so badly.

"He is sounding like a psycho." Meg made a face. "What is his problem? He is on such a power trip. Does he expect you to drop everything for him just because he says so?"

"I think he does."

"Yet he can fuck other women and even marry someone else." Meg's voice was passionate. "What an arrogant asshole."

"He said he was going to dump Maria." I stared at her with my heart thudding as I remembered his words. "He said she didn't mean anything to him."

"Did he dump her?" Meg bit her lip. "Not to be mean, but isn't that what they all say? Actions speak louder than words, and to me, it looks like he's just playing a game with you."

"I want the truth." I sighed. "And he also said Matt is Maria's brother."

"What the fuck?" Meg's jaw dropped open. "That cannot be a coincidence."

"I don't know." I sipped some more wine. "He fell asleep after sex and then when I woke up he was gone."

"Text him back and tell him you want to see him, but only if he is going to prepare some answers."

"Really?" I frowned. "Maybe I can ask him over the phone."

"No." She shook her head. "You'll know if he's telling the truth by the look in his eyes."

"That's true, I suppose."

"This shit is crazy." Meg yawned. "This is really crazy."

"I told you." I laughed, though I didn't think it was funny. I was about to text Brandon back when my phone rang. "Oh, shit. It's him. Should I answer?"

"No." She shook her head. "Let him wait it out." She smiled evilly. "And actually, don't text him until tomorrow. Let him stew a little bit."

"Oh, Meg." I put the phone on the table and sighed. "Why does life have to be so complicated?"

"Men make it that way." She jumped up and we both laughed as the phone started ringing again. "Let's go to bed. Leave the phone out here, so you aren't tempted to answer."

"Night, Meg." I gave her a quick hug before walking into my room and collapsing onto the bed. I was exhausted, mentally and emotionally, and I fell into a deep, uncomfortable sleep right away.

***

I woke up late the next day, momentarily forgetting that everything was not right in my world. I stretched languorously in the bed and yawned. Even though I'd slept for a long time, I was still tired.

"Katie." Meg knocked on my door. "Are you awake?"

"Yeah," I called out. "Come in."

Meg slowly opened the door and walked into the room. She had a weird look on her face, and I sat up to see what was going on.

"What's up?"

"You have a—" She started talking, but then Brandon suddenly appeared behind her.

"Good morning, Katie." His voice was gruff and his eyes looked at me manically. His hair was scruffy and it looked like he hadn't shaved in a couple of days.

"What are you doing here, Brandon?"

"I thought I told you to wait in the living room," Meg said at the same time. Brandon didn't even acknowledge her question or mine as he walked farther into the room and looked around.

"I called you." His voice was accusing. "And I texted you. I told you to call me back."

"I was in bed."

"Sure." His eyes were angry. "How was your early night?"

"It was fine." I blushed and looked at Meg for support. It was so much easier to tell myself to not give a shit, but now he was here in front of me and all I wanted to do was kiss him and pull him down to the bed.

Meg spoke up. "You don't own her. You can't just barge in here and question her."

"Why? Because only lawyers can question?" He looked back at Meg with a sarcastic face. "Or can unemployed

176

lawyers still question?"

"I—oh, you are so rude." Meg glared at him and then at me before striding out of the room. "Thanks for telling him my business."

"I didn't!" I called after her and frowned. "How did you know Meg lost her job?" I narrowed my eyes as I looked at Brandon, who was staring down at me. His nostrils were flaring as he studied my face.

"Where were you last night?" He sat on the bed next to me, pulled the sheets down, and surveyed my body.

"What are you doing?" I pulled the sheets back up.

"I was checking to see if you were wearing any clothes."

"How dare you!" I pushed his chest to get him off of the bed, but he didn't move.

"Oh, I dare all right." He glared at me and his fingers played with my hair. "Your hair looks like you've been through a washing machine. Rough night?"

"My night was fine."

"Your lips don't look battered." His fingers traced along my lips and he smiled. "You didn't fuck anyone last night."

"What are you talking about?" I glared at him again.

"Nothing." His eyes glittered at me. "It's nothing I can't fix."

"What are you fixing?"

"I missed you last night." He changed the subject. "I wanted to see you."

"Well, I was busy."

"You're never too busy for me."

"Sorry, but that's not true." I turned away from him. "Why are you here, Brandon?"

"Because I want to make love to you." His fingers gripped my face and turned it toward him so that we were staring into each other's eyes. "My body is craving your touch. My mouth is craving your taste. My fingers and my dick are craving your pussy."

177

"You're so crude," I mumbled in a daze against his lips. I felt myself growing wet at his words and hated myself for being so intensely attracted to this man.

"I'm not going to make love to you now." His lips pressed against mine and my body melted into him automatically. "I'm not going to suck on your nipples as if they were little candies made for my mouth. I'm not going to eat you like you were a Sunday dinner and I'm not going to take you on a roller coaster ride." He grinned as his fingers played with my hair and I breathed heavily against his lips. "I'm not going to do any of that right now."

"Oh." I couldn't say anything else. His tongue plunged into my mouth and my fingers found his hair as we kissed. We kissed each other eagerly and hungrily, our lips dancing a mambo as our tongues waltzed. He tasted sweet as always, and my fingers ran across the stubble of his face lightly. I moaned as we kissed and I thought about the stubble tickling me in my private place. I wanted him badly. My body couldn't resist his touch.

"Now, now, Katie." He pulled away from me slightly as my fingers worked their way to the front of his pants. "I told you, there will be no sex right now. But tonight, my dear… Tonight is a different story."

"What's going on tonight?" I gazed into his eyes and a little whimper escaped as he cupped my breast.

"Tonight, I'm taking you on a little adventure."

"What adventure?"

"It's a surprise." He grinned at me.

"I'm not going." I shook my head. "We need to talk."

"We can talk, but tonight we will have some fun as well." He grinned at me. "Wear a dress or a short skirt."

"Why?" My heart was beating fast now.

"You'll see." His eyes glittered and he leaned in to kiss me again.

"That's not fair." I shook my head. "You can't just come here and demand I go out with you tonight when you won't tell me where and you won't give me any other information."

"I'll tell you two things." He grinned at me wickedly. "If you do one thing for me?"

"What's that?"

"Ride me," he mumbled against my lips, and I frowned.

"I thought you said no sex."

"I don't want you to ride my cock," he laughed as he squeezed my breasts.

"I don't get it then," I moaned and pushed myself into his hands.

"I want you to ride my face."

"What?" My eyes widened.

"I know you like the stubble." He grinned at me wickedly. "And my tongue. I need to taste you before I leave."

"But what about you?" I whispered, feeling excited.

"I'll come tonight." He laughed and his eyes hardened slightly. "Tonight, you will ride me again. But that time, it will be my cock and I will have the best orgasm of my life."

"I guess." I shivered slightly. "I'm not agreeing to anything until you tell me what you have to say."

"I told you that Matt and Maria are brother and sister, right?"

"Uh huh." I sat up straight and stared at him intently. Was I finally going to get the information I always wanted?

"Their dad, Will, used to work for me. He was a private investigator for my dad's company, and that's how I met him. He was a good guy. He helped me in a lot of ways before I met you and after I met you. He had a heart attack a few years ago."

"I'm sorry."

"It's okay," he sighed. "He left me a note asking me to take care of his daughter, Maria, and to continue supporting his business, which his son, Matt, took over."

"Oh," I frowned. "I thought Matt was a journalist."

"He is a journalist." Brandon sighed. "But he grew up

in the family business, so he was able to be a private investigator as well."

"Oh." I was still confused. I didn't really understand how any of it added up.

"Right after her father died, Maria's fiancé dumped her and she attempted to commit suicide." Brandon looked at me with concern in his eyes "Matt came to me and asked me if I would become engaged to her as a way to help her mentally, and I agreed." He sighed. "It was stupid of me. I don't know what I was thinking. We should have just gotten her a therapist. But I figured, what could it hurt? It seemed to make her happy to be in a fake engagement and she didn't demand anything of me."

"So you didn't sleep with her?" I asked slowly, and he nodded.

"I told you I didn't sleep with her." He spoke angrily "I don't love her and we have never had sex. She's not the love of my life."

"So she's not Harry's mother?"

"No." Brandon shook his head and stared at me. I wanted to ask him who was then. Who was the lady he had a kid with? But I was scared and jealous. I didn't want to think about him having a baby with someone else.

"So you don't love Maria?"

"No." He shook his head. "I've never loved her."

"I see." My stomach flipped at his words. Did that mean that I had a shot? Or was I fooling myself? If he found out what I'd done, would he still be interested in seeing me? "So you paid Matt to give you information about me after I started working for you?"

"Something like that." His eyes glazed over. "That's enough talking for now."

"But I wanted to know—" I started, but he placed his finger in my mouth.

"Shhh." He grinned as I sucked on it slowly. He pulled the sheets down and pulled me up toward him before pulling his finger out of my mouth. "Come here," he growled as he tore off my t-shirt off and saw that I wasn't wearing a bra or panties. "You make me so hard, Katie."

I laughed at the expression on his face, which seemed to make him happy because he covered me with kisses as he laid down on the bed next to me. He lifted me up gently and placed me on his chest, and I quickly went to undo his belt buckle.

"No." He shook his head as his fingers pushed my ass so that my whole body was closer and closer to his face. "My clothes stay on."

"But," I protested, suddenly feeling self-conscious. I was sitting high on his chest now, my legs spread-eagled on both sides of him. I could feel his breath on my pussy and every part of me was tingling in sweet anticipation.

"No buts." He grinned and then lifted my ass up slightly. I shifted forward onto my knees and hovered over his mouth before looking down to make sure I wasn't smothering him. His eyes sparkled at me before his arms pulled my thighs down roughly and I was sitting directly on his face. My eyes widened for two seconds and then I gripped the headboard as his tongue slowly licked my pussy lips. My body buckled slightly as I felt him sucking on my clit while his stubble gently tickled me. My body started trembling and I moved back and forth on him gently, loving the feel of him against me. I felt his tongue lapping up my wetness before slowly entering me. In that moment his tongue felt just as magnificent as his cock, and I closed my eyes, delighting in the waves of pleasure as they crashed over me. His hands gripped my ass and he slowly moved me back and forth on his face as his mouth devoured me. I screamed as I felt an orgasm overtaking my body. I shuddered on top of him as I came, but Brandon didn't stop licking and teasing me. Instead he increased the motion of his tongue and I moved my hips more urgently on his face as I felt a second orgasm building up.

"Oh, Brandon!" I screamed as I rode his face,

forgetting to be gentle. My second orgasm built up even higher, and as the waves of pleasure tore through my body, I almost forgot who I was. I rolled onto the bed next to him and closed my eyes, trying not to move as I lay there feeling satiated and spent.

"Until tonight, my love." Brandon jumped off of the bed and kissed me lightly on the cheeks. "I'll see you tonight." He walked out of my room with a confident swagger and I groaned into my pillow. I had no idea what he had planned, but I knew that I was in for one hell of a night.

I smiled to myself as I thought about Brandon and what he had said about Maria and Matt. Maybe I was going to be luckier than I thought. Maybe I was actually in it for a lot longer than one night. I sighed as I thought about everything I had left to tell him. I would tell him all my secrets at the end of the night. And then he could make up his mind once and for all. We were either going to make it work or we weren't. But I couldn't keep going on like this. I would drive myself crazy. I couldn't allow my body and my brain to keep fighting like this. One of them had to win out.

***

"You look hot." Meg attempted a whistle as I exited my bedroom to wait for Brandon.

"So do you." I blinked at her. "Where are you off to?"

"I got a call from the private club." She smiled. "They want me to come in for an interview. The owner is back from some business trip or something."

"Uhm, that doesn't explain the sexy outfit," I laughed.

"I figured men will buy more alcohol from sexy girls." She grinned at me. "I want to show them I can be sexy."

"You're going to go to work like that?"

"No," she giggled. "But they don't need to know that. I'm going to go to the interview like this, and if I get the job, I'll dress regularly. What are they going to say? 'Hey, you bait-and-switched us at the interview'?"

"I guess." I laughed. "You're the lawyer, you know better than me."

"Haha, well, you're the sex queen." Meg's eyes laughed at me. "I need to get some makeup tips from you. You look hot."

"Well, you know. We're not in college anymore." I grinned and paused as we heard a knock on the door.

"How does he get up here without us buzzing him in?" Meg looked at me in confusion.

"He owns the building." I made a face.

"And that explains how we got into this building." Meg laughed and shook her head. "I always wondered how we got approved."

"Oh, wow. I never even thought about that." I stared at her, my mind buzzing.

Bang, bang.

"I can hear you girls talking. Don't make me open the door myself." Brandon's voice carried through the door and I walked to open it slowly.

"Hey," I said shyly, grinning at him as his eyes popped open. He stared at my partially exposed breasts and then down to my heavily exposed legs.

"You look amazing." He looked back up at me and I could see the desire in his eyes.

"Amazing enough for you to tell me where we're going?"

He smiled at me and licked his lips as he cocked his head to the side. "Nearly."

"Whatever," I pouted and he laughed.

"Hello, Meg."

"Hi, Brandon." She nodded at him. I could tell she still didn't really like him.

"Where are you off to?"

"A private club." She shrugged. "I've got an interview."

"Oh?" He frowned. "What club?"

"I don't know. It's just called The Club, from what I know."

"The Club?" He stilled and then gave me a quick look. "Hmm. Why are you going to interview there?"

"To get a job as a bartender." She rolled her eyes.

"I thought you were a lawyer."

"Well, I'm taking a break." She pulled on her coat. "And I'm leaving now."

"Wait." Brandon grabbed her arm and paused. "I don't think you should go. If it's the club I'm thinking of, it's not for you."

"I don't need your advice, thanks." She pulled away from him and gave me a smile. "Have a good night, Katie. If you need anything, just call." She gave him a glare. "And if you do anything to hurt my friend, I will cut your balls off." And then she gave him a huge smile and left.

"Well, she doesn't hold back, does she?" He raised an eyebrow at me and I laughed.

"You shouldn't try to tell her what to do. You don't have some special power over every woman, you know."

"I don't?" He winked at me and I hit him in the shoulder.

"How did you know she got fired?" I looked up at him carefully.

"Oh, Katie. Do we have to talk about this now?" He sighed and I nodded. "I know the partners at her old firm. I gave them a call."

"But why?" I held my breath, my heart beating fast.

"I had a feeling you were going to leave the training in San Francisco and quit. I couldn't let that happen. I knew you wouldn't quit if your best friend and roommate had been fired."

"Oh, Brandon." My face paled at his words. Inside I felt both excited and annoyed. How could he have done that to Meg? "She loved that job."

"I'll give them a call next week." His eyes burned into mine. "She'll get her job back."

"Are you sure?"

"Yeah," he nodded. "I don't want her working at the club."

"Why not?"

"If it's the club I'm thinking about, I don't think it's a good idea." His eyes darkened for a moment. "It's not a good idea at all."

"Okay," I shrugged. "So are we going now?"

"Sure, my eager beaver." He laughed and pulled me toward him before kissing me hard. I melted into his chest, and his hands rested lightly on my ass before slowly pulling the back of my dress up. His fingers caressed my ass and he gasped as he realized I had no panties on. "You are a naughty girl."

"I wanted to be accommodating." I grinned and pressed myself into his erection as he growled against my ear.

"I'm going to blindfold you, Katie," He whispered in my ear. "And I'm going to put earmuffs on your ears. I don't want you to see or hear anything. I want every part of your body to be focused on me as you take me."

"As I take you?"

"Remember my lap dance fantasy?" he whispered as his fingers teased me. "I want you to pretend you're a stripper and fuck me."

"How can I do that with a blindfold and earmuffs?" I shook my head.

"You'll find a way." He grinned at me. "When we get to the location, I'll kiss you to let you know you can start."

"I don't know." I shook my head. "This sounds awkward."

"Do it for me, Katie." He kissed me again. "I want to own your body tonight. Please me and I will please you."

"Fine." I grinned up at him. "But tomorrow morning, we need to talk. A serious talk. Do you hear me?"

"Fine." He kissed my lips one more time. "Tomorrow we shall talk."

He pulled away from me, took a blindfold out of his pocket, and placed it over my eyes. I was enveloped in darkness and suddenly felt very nervous. I had no idea where we were going, and I didn't know what to expect. He then placed a pair of earmuffs over my ears and all sound was gone as well. I held on to his arm as he escorted me out of the door and into the elevator. I took a deep breath and tried to calm my nerves as we got into the back of a car. Brandon stroked my leg as we drove and I leaned into him. I had no idea where we were going, but I was starting to get excited.

About twenty minutes later, Brandon escorted me out of the back of the car and we walked for about five minutes before he took me into a building. I wasn't even sure where we were and if he was opening any doors or what since we stopped every few seconds for him to do something. Then he picked me up and carried me, and before I knew it, I was being placed on a lush velvet couch. The material was soft underneath me and I wondered if we were in his apartment. I so wanted to pull off the blindfold and the earmuffs, but I knew he would be upset, and part of me enjoyed the thrill of it all. I felt Brandon slide down next to me and his thigh felt warm against mine. I waited in sweet anticipation for him to kiss me, and when it came, I climbed eagerly into his lap.

I straddled him and grinned against his mouth as I felt his erection pressing into me. He kissed me hard and his tongue danced along with the beat of my hips as I gyrated on him. His hands pushed my ass against him harder and I groaned as he broke the kiss and sucked on my neck. I continued moving back and forth on him like I was some sort of dirty stripper and I moaned against his hair as his fingers slipped between my legs. His head then moved farther down my neck until his teeth were pulling the top of my dress to the side. Then I felt his lips on my nipple and I ran my hands to his hair and pulled.

I continued gyrating on him for about a minute before

reaching down to let his cock out. It felt hard and long, and I sat up a little bit before sliding down on him and taking him inside of me. His fingers gripped my waist and moved me up and down on him. I cried out as I bounced on top of him and rubbed my breasts in his face. I could feel that he was about to orgasm at the same time I was, and I squeezed his shoulders as he bit down on my nipple. I moved faster and faster and screamed as I climaxed on top of him. I could feel his body shuddering as he came in me and ripped the blindfold off of my face.

My eyes couldn't even focus as my orgasm was so intense, but I soon realized that I was staring into the street. I looked around and realized that not only was I not in Brandon's apartment, I was in a store somewhere, on a couch in the corner of the room. I looked around the dark room and discovered I was in a bar. I could see a couple of people across the way looking at us, and I froze on top of him. Brandon looked down at me with dark eyes and kissed me again as he slipped the earmuffs off. I was about to ask him where we were when I heard a voice behind me.

"I'm going to have to ask you both to leave this instant," a familiar male voice spoke up and I froze. Brandon's hands were still on my waist, holding me down on him, and I was unable to get off of his lap.

"We'll be gone in a moment." Brandon's voice was terse. "I'm sure you understand that it will be better if I finish in her rather than on the couch."

"Dude, if you don't want me to call the cops, you better get out of here." The man's voice was shocked. "You and your girl need to leave my bar now."

And then it hit me. I knew where I was. I twisted my head and saw the Getting Lucky sign on the door. My heart froze as I turned to look at the man who was speaking. It was the bartender from the other night. My face turned red as he stared at me, and his eyes widened in shock.

"Katie." He took a step back and looked at me with a disappointed face.

"I, uh…" I stammered, not knowing what to say.

"We need to go, Katie." Brandon's voice was pleased as his hands released their grip on my waist. He made a show of pulling the back of my dress down and letting his fingers hover on my pussy for a few seconds as he rubbed it gently. His hands then went to the front of my dress and pinched my nipples before adjusting the top. He then slid me off of him and jumped up, pulling me up with him. "This is for your inconvenience." He dropped some bills on the table and nodded at the bartender. "Let's go."

He grabbed my hand and pulled me with him out of the bar. I looked at the ground in shame as we exited quickly. My blood was boiling and I didn't know what to do.

"You're mine, Katie," he whispered in my ear as we left the bar. "I expect you to never come back to this bar." His eyes glittered as he stared at me. "You better not lie to me and see that man ever again."

CHAPTER 4
BRANDON

Katie's eyes were wide with shock and anger, and I knew that I had pushed her too far. I was scared inside, and I knew my jealousy had allowed me to cross a line I shouldn't have.

"How dare you!" She yanked her hand away from me. "Why did you do this?"

"I wanted to show the bartender that he could never have you." The words sounded weak coming from my mouth. I knew that I sounded like some sort of caveman. But I didn't know how to explain to her how much she meant to me and how badly I had hurt the night before when Matt had called me. I'd gone down to the bar after I'd gotten off of the phone with Matt with intentions of letting the bartender know that he needed to back off. But then I'd thought, *What if he takes that as a reason to really start pursuing her?* What if I saw them kissing or doing something even worse? I would have gone crazy. I'd pictured the blood in my mind and had texted and called Katie all night. But she hadn't answered the phone or texted me back. She had all but confirmed my fears, and all I could think of was her with another man, letting him touch her and kiss her. It had driven me crazy. And in my mind,

189

there was only one way for me to make sure that she never hooked up with him. He had to know and she had to know that she was mine.

"Why?" She shook her head and her eyes were devoid of light. "I barely even know him."

"You kissed him!" I almost shouted, feeling angry again as I thought about her lips on his.

"How do you know that?" She paused and her eyes widened. "Are you having me followed?"

"No." I shook my head quickly.

"Then how did you know I knew him?"

"You told me you kissed him. You told me!" I shouted and tried to grab her hands.

"I didn't tell you where I was." She pulled away from me. "Are you some freaking stalker, Brandon? Really, you're a creeper and a stalker."

"I know you came here last night as well." I couldn't stop myself. "You told me you were staying in, but you came here to see him again."

"What?" Her mouth dropped open in shock. "How do you know I came here?"

"So you don't deny it?" My heart broke as I realized that Matt hadn't been lying. "You did come here to see him last night."

"I came back last night because I forgot to pay the last time I was here." She looked at me angrily. "The last time I was here, I ordered a bunch of drinks and ran out because when *he* kissed me, all I could think about was you. I remembered that I hadn't paid, so I came back yesterday to pay what I owed."

"You didn't come back because you wanted him?" My heart beat faster and I grinned at her, happy.

"No, you fucking asshole." Her eyes glittered at me. "You just humiliated me for nothing."

"I'm sorry, I didn't mean to—"

"Oh shut up!" she screamed. "I'm done, you hear? I'm done. I can't take this anymore, Brandon. You use me and treat me like some sort of two-dollar whore. I'm not going to let you do this to me anymore. I don't want to see you ever again. You're a fucking stalker. How dare you have me followed!"

"I didn't have you followed." I grabbed ahold of her. "I swear it. Matt was in here last night and he saw you, and we put two and two together."

"How would he know to put anything together? Why would he even call you and tell you that? Do you know how crazy that sounds, Brandon? My ex-boyfriend called my other ex-boyfriend to tell him that I'm at a bar."

"He said you were flirting."

"So what? I can flirt with anyone I like."

"You kissed him as well." I knew the words sounded childish coming out of my mouth.

"I can kiss him if I want to, Brandon, you don't own me. We're not even together."

"I haven't been with anyone since you, Katie, and I know you haven't either."

"What?" She froze and she stared at me before hitting me in the chest. "How do you know who I have and haven't been with? How long have you been spying on me? Oh my God, Brandon. Are you fucking crazy?"

"Wait." My heart froze at her words. "It's not like that, Katie. I love you."

"No, you don't." She shook her head. "I don't even know if you ever did. You know I never stopped loving you, Brandon. I've been thinking about the man you were when we met and I've dreamed of the day that I would get to see you again. I hoped that we'd be able to move on from what happened seven years ago. I thought that if I saw you again, and you saw me, we would have another connection. And yeah," she laughed hysterically, "I looked you up and tried to see what you were up to and who you dated. And yeah, I bumped into Matt on purpose because I wanted to know more about you. I wanted to be around you again and see if we had a shot at another chance. What

I did was wrong. I snooped and I did things I'm ashamed of. But I did it because I thought I loved you. I did it because I thought that maybe we still had a shot."

"We do! We—" I started, but she cut me off.

"But you're not the man I thought you were, Brandon. I thought you were strong and kind and compassionate. I thought you were loving and protective. But you're not. You're just a fucking asshole, like every other man who's on a power trip. Well, you know what? You can fuck off. I'm done. You can't tell me who I can and can't fuck. If I want to go back into the bar and fuck the bartender now, I will. And you can't stop me. Do you hear me? I'm not your possession. You do not own me. You cannot humiliate me and tell me you think it's okay because you were jealous. That's not how life goes, Brandon. At least not for me." She stared at me for a moment, and I watched as tears fell down her face. It reminded me of the day we had broken up when she was at Columbia University. I stood still as she stared at me waiting for me to speak, but I didn't know what to say.

She turned around and walked away, and I watched her hobbling. I felt sick to my stomach at what I'd done and at her words. She didn't love me anymore. I'd pushed her too far. It was over. A part of me was resigned to watching her leave. This was my life and my destiny. I was meant to be alone.

As I watched her walk away, I thought back to that day seven years ago. The day that created a cut in my heart so deep that I was sure it would never be repaired. I remembered standing in the front of the class, waiting for her to look up and see me. I'd seen her right away—I had some sort of Katie sensor that knew where she was immediately whenever she was near me. Her eyes had widened in shock and fear as she glanced at me.

I was surprised that I had been able to keep it together as I gave my speech. I knew as I spoke to the group of eager freshmen that it was over. I'd given her so many chances, but she'd proven to me that she wasn't ready. My heart had broken when she'd thought we still had a chance, when she'd thought I'd forgiven her for her duplicity.

I hadn't wanted to hurt her or to break her. I just wanted her to feel the pain I had felt. I'd given her so many chances, and she had never come through. While I fucked her over the dumpster, I felt like a sick fuck. A perverted wannabe. I wanted her to scream and to shout at me then. I wanted her to realize why I had to do what I did. She was too young. She didn't know the world and she didn't know her own mind.

So I'd fucked her and walked away and then I'd watched her collapse onto the ground in tears. And I'd just walked away with my heart in my mouth and my head pounding with hate.

I waited for her to show up the next day, to tell me she was sorry and that she loved me and wanted to make it work. But she never came back. She never called and I never called and that was it. The end. It was so easy and simple and it was as if we'd never been together. Only the hole in my heart never grew back.

I'd hired Will to follow her and keep an eye on her. Not every day, but just to make sure everything was okay. He reported back to me once a week and I would read his reports and study his photographs while lying on the bed and staring at a photograph we'd taken together on a trip to the museum.

When Will told me that he thought she was sick, I nearly called her. Enough was enough. I couldn't stand back while the love of my life was sick. But then Will got the hospital records and I found out the truth. At first I was excited and then a little scared. I knew she would call me then. How could she not? I knew I could have called, but I wanted her to reach out first. I wanted her to make the decision that she wanted to be with me because she loved me. I didn't want her to feel trapped. She was so young, and I didn't want to be the guy who did that.

But she never called, and my world grew bleaker and darker. She never called and I never called, and eventually it was over and both of our lives had changed. I'd hated her and loved her, both at the same time.

As I stood there watching her walk away again, tears running down her face, I knew that I couldn't make the same mistake twice. This time, I was going to fight for her. This time, I wasn't going to just let her go. I wasn't perfect—I knew that. But I still loved her, and I had to try again.

"Wait!" I shouted as I ran after her. I grabbed ahold of her shoulders and stopped her. "Wait a minute."

"What?" She looked at me coldly and I took a deep breath before speaking again.

"I know you don't want to see me again. I understand that."

"Good." She glared at me and shook my hand off of her shoulder.

"But what about your son?" I paused as her face turned white. "Do you want to see your son?"

"What are you talking about?" she whispered, and I grabbed her arms to keep her from falling.

"I know you were pregnant, Katie." I stared into her wide eyes. "I don't know how you could give him up without telling me, but I know."

"I, I..." She blinked rapidly and her eyes glazed over. "I'm sorry I didn't tell you."

"I understand why." I pulled her toward me. "You were young. You didn't know what to do. I understand."

"Do you hate me?" Tears started flowing from her eyes again. "I'm sorry I never told you. I didn't know what to do after what happened, and then I found out I was pregnant. I was so scared. I was just eighteen and a freshman. I had no one to turn to."

"I could never hate you, Katie." I rubbed the back of her head. "I shouldn't have ended things the way that I did."

"I've always regretted it, you know." Her eyes glazed over. "I wish I'd kept him. He would have been a piece of you that I would have always had. He's still in my heart."

"I know."

"I love him," she cried. "I hate you, Brandon. I hate you for doing this to me."

"I'm sorry, Katie. I made a mistake." I sighed. "I've made a lot of mistakes. And I'm sorry about tonight. You have to believe that. You have to believe me. Please. I didn't mean to hurt you. I can't live without you."

"I don't know what to say." She shook her head as if to clear it.

"You don't have to say anything. I'm not going to force you to give me another chance. I'm not going to predicate anything on our getting back together." I took a deep breath. I couldn't lose her again.

"I don't know what you want, Brandon."

"I don't want anything. Do you want to meet Harry?"

"Harry?" She gave me a weird look.

"He's your son, Katie." I stared down at her and smiled. "Harry's our son." Katie's eyes gazed at me in confusion, before she finally understood what I was saying. I held on tightly to her as she collapsed into my arms in shock.

CHAPTER 5
KATIE

Sleep eluded me as I lay in bed. I stared at the clock on the nightstand and sighed. It was four a.m. I still had four hours before Brandon was going to pick me up and take me to meet Harry.

"Harry," I said slowly in the dark. "Harry," I said again and smiled. I was going to meet my son. My son.

It didn't even seem real. I was scared and I was excited, both at the same time. He was a little over six years old now. My heart broke as I thought about the six years of his life I had lost. Six years I would never get back. Six years Brandon had devoted to him. Our son.

I didn't know how to think about Brandon anymore. I still loved him; I knew I probably would always love him. But I wasn't sure I could deal with his style of crazy. He was too hard for me to figure out and his actions were too extreme. I cringed as I thought about the incident in the bar. I could still remember the hot burn on my face as I had made eye contact with the bartender. He had looked disgusted and shocked, so different than the teasing sweetness of the previous two days.

What Brandon had done was unacceptable. But his revelation after the incident had taken my breath away. I couldn't believe that he had known all this time that we'd had a baby. That he was now raising our baby. My hand flew to my mouth as I cried out. He wasn't a baby anymore. I didn't have a baby. He was a young boy. I'd missed the first years of his life. I felt tears forming in my eyes as I thought about everything I'd lost.

Beep beep.

My phone went off and I grabbed it quickly.

"Hey." It was Brandon.

I texted back quickly. "Hey."

"What are you doing?"

"Sleeping."

"Want to talk?"

"No."

"I can't sleep."

"That sucks for you."

"I'm thinking about what an ass I am."

"Good for you."

"My fingers are getting tired typing. Can I call you?"

I lay there staring at the phone. I wanted to talk to him, but I didn't.

"Did I lose you? :(" he texted back again and I smiled.

"No, I'm still sleep-texting."

"I knew you were smart :)"

"I did go to Columbia, you know!"

"I know. A little birdie told me."

"Haha."

"What are you wearing?"

"Nothing."

"What? I want a photo."

"I meant none of your business."

"Not fair."

"What are you wearing?" I shook my head as I typed.

"Boxers."

"Oh."

"I can send you a pic if you want! :) :)"

"I don't want."

":("

I snuggled into the sheets and smiled as I waited for his next text. I held the phone in my hands eagerly and felt my smile fade as I realized that he might not text me back again.

Beep beep.

"Miss me yet?"

"No." I smiled to myself again.

"You have to admit that it was slightly hot."

"It was not hot." I glared at the phone.

"I made you come."

"You always make me come!"

"Score 1 for me. :)"

"Idiot."

"I love you."

"I'm going back to sleep now. Bye." I put the phone down and closed my eyes. My heart was beating fast as I thought about his words. I picked the phone back up and stared at the screen. I didn't know what to think or feel. Did he really love me?

Then the phone rang and I bit my lower lip. I didn't know whether or not I should answer.

"I thought you weren't going to answer." His voice was soft as he spoke into the phone.

"I guess you thought wrong," I whispered into the phone and closed my eyes.

"You sound sexy when you're sleeping."

"Really?" I giggled and faked a snore.

"That's even sexier."

"You're not allowed to call me sexy."

"Is it too soon?"

"Huh?"

"I guess I'm still in trouble. I'll save the sexy talk for next week."

"You'll still be in trouble next week, Brandon." I shook my head. "I'm still mad at you."

"You can't stay mad at me."

"You think?"

"I hope." His voice was warm and husky. "I wish I were with you right now."

"So you can make love to me again?"

"No. So I can hold you in my arms and kiss you."

"Uh huh."

"And smell you."

"Smell me?" I frowned and lifted my arm up to see if my armpit smelled.

"You always smell like gardenias." I could hear the smile in his voice.

"Really?" I sniffed again and all I could smell was a faint sniff of the popcorn I'd made when I got home.

"Yeah. When I'm with you, I feel like I'm home."

"Oh." My heart melted at his words. "I'm still mad at you."

"I'm excited for you to meet, Harry." His tone changed. "I think you'll like him."

"I'm a bit scared," I admitted honestly. "What if he doesn't like me?"

"He'll like you," Brandon laughed. "Don't be scared."

"I've never been around little kids before," I mumbled, though that wasn't what was worrying me. I was scared that I wouldn't feel anything for him. I was scared I would see him and it would be as if I were looking at just another child. And even worse, I was scared we wouldn't have any sort of connection.

"You will be a natural."

"I hope so." I yawned.

"I should let you sleep." Brandon sounded sad. "It's late."

"Just a few more minutes," I mumbled, not wanting to get off of the phone as yet.

"You never answered me, you know," he said.

"Answered what?"

"I told you I loved you." He sounded unsure of himself. "You didn't say anything."

"I didn't know what to say," I answered honestly, feeling confused.

"You think I'm a jerk." He sighed. "I'm not perfect, Katie. I've made my mistakes."

"You can say that again." I rolled my eyes in the dark at his words and turned over in the bed.

"I'm glad you answered the phone." His voice was soft again. "I needed to hear your voice tonight. I couldn't sleep. I needed to know you would still talk to me."

"I don't hate you, Brandon." I sighed. "I just don't want anything from you."

"You think I'm an egomaniac."

"I know you're an egomaniac."

"I suppose it doesn't help if I tell you I want to make you come."

"What?" I gasped into the phone.

"I want you to fall asleep thinking about me inside of you." His voice was silky. "I want to make you come."

"Well, it's a pity you're not here," I murmured into the phone as I imagined him kissing my neck. I let out a little whimper as I imagined him playing with my breasts at the same time.

"What are you doing?" His voice was alert and I knew he had heard my whimper.

"Nothing."

"Play with yourself for me."

"No." I shook my head, but my hands rubbed my stomach.

"I'm thinking about you right now," He whispered into the phone. "I'm imagining your hands soft and cold on my cock, gliding up and down slowly, trying to tease me. I'm imagining your mouth taking over for your hands and your lips sucking down on me, tasting me and biting me lightly." He groaned and I froze as I listened to him.

"What are you doing?" I whispered, waiting for him to continue. His talk was making me feel horny and I shifted in the bed uncomfortably.

"Nothing," he groaned. "It can wait."

"Okay." I was disappointed that he had stopped before he had really gotten started.

"I'm not going to have phone sex with a girl who's sleeping," he joked into the phone. "I want you to remember me in the morning."

"Uh huh."

"But don't worry, it will be your face I picture when we get off the phone."

"What?" I squeaked out.

"Nothing, beautiful Katie," he sighed. "Get some sleep. I'll be picking you up in a few hours."

"Okay," I sighed, not wanting to get off of the phone.

"What's wrong?" he questioned me and I was quiet. "Katie."

"Nothing."

"Do you want me to stay on the phone?" he whispered.

"No," I lied.

"I remember when we first started dating. You always wanted me to stay on the phone with you." He laughed. "I'm not sure how either of us got anything done with all those marathon calls."

"We didn't have that many," I giggled as I remembered those first days.

"We spoke on the phone every night. You talked my ear off going on about books and TV shows." He laughed. "But it was all worth it when I heard your sweet little snores as you fell asleep."

"I don't snore."

"I'm afraid you do."

"No one has ever told me I snored," I protested.

"How many men have you slept with?" His tone changed, and I could hear the jealousy. I felt all warm inside as he spoke and I knew that I was just as dysfunctional as him.

"I'm not answering the question."

"I know the answer already," he laughed.

"You're a creep."

"I didn't stop you from dating anyone."

"I know," I sighed. "Do you ever think about the days before we broke up? The days before I moved in? The first days?"

"All the time."

"They were good, weren't they?"

"The very best."

"Thank you for taking Harry," I whispered.

"I love you, Katie." His voice was stronger this time. "And I love Harry more than life itself."

"You're a good dad."

"I got one thing right." He sighed. "Stay the night tomorrow."

"No."

"Think about it."

"Okay, I'll think about it."

"Sweet dreams, Katie."

"Sweet dreams, Brandon." I waited for him to hang up before I put down the phone. "You're still there," I whispered, and he laughed.

"I'm hoping I get to hear the snores of an angel again."

"You want me to fall asleep on the phone?"

"I want you to fall asleep in my arms, but the phone will have to do tonight."

"Night, Brandon." I closed my eyes and snuggled into my pillow, the phone pressed against my ear. I lay there listening to the sound of his breathing and it comforted me. Before I knew it, I had fallen into a deep sleep and I had dreams filled with Brandon, me, and babies.

***

"Don't worry, Katie. It'll be fine." Brandon squeezed my hand as we walked up to the front door of his dad's house. "Just remember, don't tell him you're his mom, please. I don't want to shock him."

"I won't tell him." I nodded. I felt hurt that Brandon didn't want Harry to know right away, but I understood slightly. "Who does he think Maria is to him?" I frowned as we waited at the door.

"He's only known Maria for the last year or so. She moved in fairly recently." Brandon sighed. "He thinks she's his babysitter."

"Oh." I bit my lower lip to stop from saying anything else.

"Hello," a sweet older lady said when she answered the door. She had platinum blond hair and a big red smile. "Brandon, you're here early." She gave him a hug and then looked at me.

"This is my friend Katie, Verna." He introduced us, and the lady known as Verna looked me over with knowing eyes.

"Katie, this is my father's girlfriend, Verna."

"Nice to meet you." I reached over to shake her hand, but she gave me a hug instead.

"It's wonderful to meet you, my girl." She smiled at me happily. "You have such pretty brown eyes."

I smiled back at her, appreciating her warmth to me, and was about to speak when I saw a little boy darting to the door.

"Daddy!" He ran into Brandon's arms, grinning. "I'm having pancakes."

"I can see that," Brandon replied with a smile, and we all laughed as Harry's face was covered in syrup.

"Do you want some pancakes, Dad?" Harry grinned and then looked at me. "Hello, I'm Harry."

"Hi, Harry. I'm Katie." I choked up slightly. "It's nice to meet you."

"Do you like to play video games?" He studied my face for a few moments.

"I'm not terribly good, but I do enjoy some."

"Then come and play Mario Kart with me. It's fine 'cause Granddad said I could play," he quickly added as he looked at his dad, and I laughed. I tried not to stare at him like a crazy woman, but I couldn't stop myself from studying him.

He was a gorgeous little boy and looked like a mini-Brandon but with my big brown eyes. His hair was dirty blond and he had a round little face that looked very dirty at the moment. Though I had a feeling that his face was always slightly dirty. His cheeks were rosy and red and he was a little plump, with his round little belly—probably from playing too many video games.

"Or we could play basketball or soccer." I smiled at him, thinking that it was time to introduce some sports into his life. I laughed inside at my maternal instincts and I saw Brandon giving me a side stare.

"I want to play basketball!" He jumped up and down. "I wanna be just like Kobe Bryant when I grow up."

"Oh?" I nodded at him and smiled. "He's a good player, all right." I knew the name, but I had no idea what basketball team he played for, and I was praying that Harry wouldn't ask me.

"Or LeBron James." He grinned. "I could be LeBron James as well."

"Well, right now you're going to be the little boy who goes and cleans his face." Brandon interrupted us and we all walked into the house. "Go and get cleaned up, Harry. Katie and I are taking you out."

"YES!" He pumped his fist. "McDonalds time."

"No, Harry." He shook his head and laughed. "I thought we could all go to a museum or something."

"Boring." Harry made a face. "I don't wanna go to a museum."

"Don't be rude." Brandon gave him a small stare and I turned my face away to stop from laughing. Brandon was a wonderful father, but it was a bit weird watching him in that role.

"I'm being honest." Harry shrugged and smiled at me. "You know that, right, Katie?"

"Yes, I do think you're being honest."

"See." He grinned at his dad.

"What would you like to do, Harry?" I asked him softly, and he turned to look at me with big adoring eyes. I thought my heart melted right then and there.

"I wanna go McDonalds and to a movie and maybe to a toy store to get some new Legos or a new game for my Wii. And then I wanna go and get some candy." He paused for a second. "But not Reese's Pieces. I don't like Reese's.

"Neither do I," I laughed happily, and Brandon gently smiled at me.

"He favors his mother in a lot of ways," He whispered in my ear. "Brown eyes, doesn't like Reese's, likes to have his own way too much." I gave him a quick look and he grinned at me before turning back to our son. "Harry, go and get cleaned up and come back downstairs please."

"Yes, Dad." Harry ran off and Verna turned to us both.

"You make a lovely couple." She smiled but walked off before I was able to deny he comment.

"She thinks we're together," I groaned and looked at Brandon.

"So?" He shrugged.

"But we're not."

"Yet." He smiled slowly and pulled me toward him. He kissed me lightly on the nose and then on the lips. "I enjoyed falling asleep with you last night."

"Uh huh." I blinked up at him, my heart beating fast.

"Falling asleep with someone is so much more intimate than having sex with them," he whispered in my ear.

"You think so?" I smiled up at him. "Then I guess you never want to have sex with me again?"

"Don't be funny," he laughed as his hands caressed my ass. "If we weren't in my dad's house right now, I'd be fucking you right here."

"Really?" I raised an eyebrow. "And it's only because

we're in your dad's house? I thought you got off on public sex."

"Argh." He groaned and his hands massaged my shoulders. "Okay, I'd fuck you here in a minute if Harry weren't here."

"I knew it."

"Does it make you feel better that you're right?" he whispered against my lips, and I leaned in and kissed him hard; this time I was going to turn him on in an awkward place. I slipped my tongue into his mouth and nibbled on his lower lip before pressing my breasts against his chest and reaching down and squeezing his hardening cock.

"Shit, Katie," he groaned against me as I unzipped him, slipped my hand inside his pants, and ran my fingers lightly over his cock. He gasped at my touch and I smiled as I continued to kiss him. As soon as I heard footsteps coming, I withdrew my hand and walked over to look at some paintings on the wall.

"Ready!" Harry ran back to the entryway and I smiled at him widely as Brandon quickly zipped himself back up.

"Well, that was fast, Son." Brandon's voice was tight, and he gave me a look filled with such lust and desire that my panties grew wet.

"Let's go play." Harry grabbed my hand. "Bye, Grandpa. Bye, Grandma Verna."

"Where's your dad?" I asked Brandon, surprised I hadn't met him.

"I think he's still in bed." He laughed. "Verna spoils him and serves him breakfast in bed every morning."

"Oh, wow."

"Let's go." Harry pulled me towards the front door.

"Don't squeeze Katie's hand off, Harry," Brandon chuckled as we walked through the front door.

"I'm not." He laughed and smiled up at me. "I'm not hurting you, am I, Katie?"

"No, Harry." I smiled down at him with love in my eyes. "You're not hurting me at all."

***

"Go up and have a bath, Harry. I'll be up in fifteen minutes to read you a bedtime story."

"Yes, Dad." Harry yawned and looked over at me. "Will I see you tomorrow, Katie?"

"If you want to." I smiled at him happily. We'd had a long day, taking him to a children's museum and then to a late lunch and back home to watch a movie together. It had been such a great day. I was a little sad that it was over.

"Yeah, let's go to McDonalds tomorrow."

"I don't know about McDonalds," I laughed, "but I'm sure we can think of something to do."

"Okay." Harry ran up the stairs, and Brandon came and sat next to me on the couch.

"You're good with him." He stared into my eyes. "You make a good mother."

"I don't know about all that." I made a face and looked around the living room. "I love your house. I didn't know you had a brownstone."

"I bought it after I got Harry." He shrugged. "I still have the apartment though. It's still intact from the days we lived together."

"How did you get Harry?" I bit my lip, but I couldn't stop myself from asking the question that had been on my mind for so long. "The adoption agency told me it was a closed adoption, but a couple in Connecticut were adopting him."

"The lady in charge of the adoption agency is an advocate for fathers' rights." His voice was low. "I went in and told her that I was the father and they didn't have my permission. We got a blood test done and I took him home."

"They can do that?"

"When you have money, you can get a lot of things

pushed through quickly." He shrugged. "I wasn't going to let my son be raised by strangers."

"You think I'm horrible, don't you?"

"No, you were just young." He shook his head and sat back. "There are so many things I think we both would have done differently if we had it to do over." He sighed. "I think that you never really realize what you've lost until it's gone." He stared at me sadly. "Sometimes, the biggest revenge is showing someone what they could have had."

"I don't know what to say." I looked away from him, my heart breaking.

"It was always you, Katie. It was only you. There's never been anyone in my life that I've wanted before. Never." He sighed and stood up. "I wish you hadn't lied to me." His eyes looked down at me and he walked away. "I'm going to go and read Harry a bedtime story now. Feel free to relax until I get back."

I sat back and stared at the rug, feeling as if I were in Wonderland. My emotions were all over the place and I didn't know which way was up and which way was down. I heard footsteps and looked up, expecting to see Brandon, but a tall, beautiful lady walked into the room instead.

"Hello," I smiled at her politely.

"You're a fool." The lady's eyes surveyed me with pity.

"Excuse me?" I sat up straight.

"I said you're a fool, Katie Raymond."

"And you are?" I asked slowly, though I was pretty sure I knew the answer.

"I'm Brandon's fiancée, Maria." She sat next to me. "I'm sure you've heard of me before."

"You were engaged to him in college as well." I nodded, letting her know I did know exactly who she was.

"College?" She laughed. "I'm not that Maria. I'm the new and better version. At least that's what Brandon tells me. The girl in college was a mistake. Like you." She cackled as she looked at me, flinging her long, dark hair behind her shoulders.

"I see." I looked away from her, not knowing what to say.

"When you fucked him, did he say my name?" Maria leaned towards me and hissed. "Did he tell you that he likes to fuck me in the car, in the shower, in the elevator, in the kitchen?"

"He told me he's never slept with you." I jumped up, angry and upset. I wanted to be away from this woman. "He told me he doesn't love you, that he only became engaged to you because of your dad."

Maria started laughing, but I could see her face turning red. "I suppose he's right about one thing. The only woman he ever really loved was Denise."

"Who?" I frowned and turned to look at her.

"Denise. She's the one who ruined him. The one he wishes every woman was like. She was a freak in the bedroom, let him do things to her that other women wouldn't even think of." Maria stood up and smiled at me. "I suppose I should feel sorry for you. You're like me. You got caught up in his lies and his spell. He doesn't love you, you know. This is just about revenge and power for him. He uses us because his true love, Denise, used him. Once you submit to him, he will be gone. Just like he was before."

"You're lying." I turned away from her, not wanting to hear anything else she had to say.

"Go to his study, turn on the TV, and press play on the DVD player." Maria shrugged and turned away from me. "He goes to his study every day and watches that video to remind himself of who he was and what he lost."

"I'm not going anywhere."

"Are you scared, little girl?" She laughed hysterically and then turned around abruptly. I watched as she left the room and the house. I stood there in shock. What was she talking about? I'd never heard of a Denise before in my life. I thought back to the last few weeks and everything that had happened. It had seemed like Brandon had been

210

deliberately trying to humiliate me and hurt me. How did I know if he really truly loved me or if this was just a game to him?

I walked to the study slowly, ashamed of myself for believing Maria's lies. *I just need to know that it's a lie,* I told myself as I entered the study and turned on the TV. It took me a few minutes to find the DVD player. It was hidden behind some books. I pressed play and waited.

The screen flashed on and I blinked. It was Brandon's bedroom in his apartment that I was looking at—the apartment I had shared with him. I stared at the screen and watched as Brandon walked in with two girls. My heart started thudding as I watched him undressing one while the other one undressed him. I felt like I couldn't breathe when they all fell to the bed together. One girl started kissing him while the other went down on him. I stumbled back until I fell into a chair, but my eyes didn't move from the screen. I watched as he played with both girls and teased them. Then one of the women left the room and it was just him and a tall blonde. A beautiful, voluptuous blonde. She sat on top of him, teasing him, and he was groaning as he played with her breasts.

"Fuck me, Denise," he groaned. "Fuck me now." She whispered something to him and he groaned again. "You know it's always been you, Denise. I don't want anyone else but you. Please, just fuck me." His hands reached to her hips and I watched as she sank down on him and rode him hard. Brandon's eyes were closed and he muttered something incomprehensible.

"Katie, where are you?" I heard Brandon's voice calling out to me from the hallway, but I couldn't speak. My tears were streaming down my face too quickly. A sob escaped from my mouth and I heard Brandon's footsteps walking towards the study.

"Katie?" He opened the door slowly. "What's wrong?"

His eyes widened in concern as he stared at me. I pointed to the TV screen as I couldn't make eye contact with him, and I heard him gasp.

"What the fuck?" He walked over to the screen and frowned as he turned it off. "How did you find this?"

"Maria told me to come in and watch it," I gulped.

"Maria was here?" He sighed and walked up to me. "That was an old video, Katie. Please don't cry. Denise was someone I knew before I met you."

"She was the love of your life." I tried not to let him see how much I was breaking inside. "You told her you wanted her and that she was the one."

"Katie, you have to believe me when I say that Denise was never the one." He shook his head angry. "I could kill Matt."

"Matt?" I looked at him and frowned.

"He must have given Maria the video." He sighed. "He's the only one with access to it, now that his father is dead."

"I don't understand."

"Katie," he sighed. "I didn't want to go into this. But before I met you, I dated a girl called Denise. She was beautiful and sexually adventurous. She liked to have a good time and so did I."

"You guys had threesomes?" I stared at him with accusing eyes and he nodded.

"I told you when I met you, Katie. I wasn't a saint. I'm a virile man. I like sex." He shrugged. "It was all before you." He sighed and then continued. "Anyways, it turned out that Denise was a high-class escort and she had targeted me with some of her colleagues. They tried to blackmail me for twenty million dollars. They were going to go to a newspaper and write a tell-all about all the kinky prostitute sex I liked." My eyes widened as he told his story and he looked at me with a sad expression. "I mean, it was true. The only part that would have been omitted was that I knew they were prostitutes. But no one would have believed me." He crouched down and grabbed my hands. "So I hired a private detective to investigate them.

212

That was how I met Will. When I met you, I really liked you, but I didn't know if I could trust my gut instincts, so I had Will follow you too. In fact, I had him follow both of us. I wanted to know what you did when you were with me and when you weren't with me, so I could be sure that you were genuine."

"I never knew that." My eyes widened, but my tears had dried up.

"I didn't want you to know." He stood up and pulled me up next to him. "You passed with flying colors. Will loved you. He thought you were perfect. His report told me you were the furthest thing from a gold digger he'd seen." He smiled at me gently. "He had just confirmed what I had already known in my heart, Katie. I'm sorry I did it. But you have to know that you are the only one I've truly loved, not Denise. Never Denise. She's nothing to me."

"Liar." We both jumped as Maria walked back into the room with an evil smile. "You're a liar, Brandon Hastings."

"Get out of here." Brandon's face was red with anger. "After all I've done for your family, you try and ruin my life."

"You're a liar, Brandon," Maria hissed as she walked up the TV and turned it on again. She rewound the DVD and pressed play. I cringed as I watched Brandon on the screen moaning in ecstasy with Denise on top of him. "Look carefully, Katie." She pointed at the screen. "For just one moment, stop thinking about your little girl pain and Brandon fucking another woman. Look at the room, Katie. What do you see?"

I tried to ignore her words, but I couldn't. I looked at the room more carefully to see what she was talking about. And then I gasped. I stared at Brandon, angry and hurt. He had lied to me. Everything had been a lie. One great big lie.

"You lied," I whispered, horrified and heartbroken. He stared back at me with an ashen face and I knew then that he knew he had been caught. I turned back to the screen and watched as Brandon made love to another woman with the photograph we'd taken together at the museum staring down at him from the night table next to the bed.

CHAPTER 6
BRANDON

I stared at Katie in dread. She'd caught me in a lie. A big lie. A lie that was more harmful than the lie she'd told me. A lie that meant I'd have to reveal everything if I was to stand a chance of gaining her total trust and love again.

"Nothing to say, Brandon?" Maria's voice was catty and delighted, and I knew that she had deliberately set this whole thing up to hurt me for ending the fake engagement.

"You need to leave. Now." I turned toward her with murder in my eyes.

"I think someone needs to protect poor, innocent Katie. Don't you, Brandon?" She laughed. "We wouldn't want her thinking this was all her fault, would we?" Her eyes narrowed at me and I grabbed her arm.

"You are to leave and never come back." I looked down at her and whispered, "If I ever see you again, I will ruin your brother's life. I will make sure he is fired from the *Wall Street Journal* and is never employed by another newspaper in New York again."

"You wouldn't do that." Her face paled at my words. I knew I had hit a sore spot. She loved her brother Matt more than anyone in the world.

"Don't test me." I pushed her toward the door. "Leave

now."

"What about Harry?" She looked at me with big eyes. "He'll miss me."

"You will never see him again." I clenched my fists as I thought about all the times I'd left him alone with her. I wanted to punch myself for being so blind as to how crazy she was.

"But you love me, Brandon," she whimpered. "You wanted to marry me."

"Maria." My voice rose and she ran out of the room. I followed her out and watched as she exited before slowly going back into the room. "I guess I'll have to change the locks," I joked as I re-entered the study, but Katie didn't smile.

I stood there, not knowing what to say or where to start.

"I guess we should talk." I cleared my throat and stared at her. I was surprised to see that she wasn't crying. "I'm sorry for lying."

"One lie begets another lie, I suppose." Her face was expressionless, and my heart froze at the lack of emotion in her tone. I could have dealt with anger, jealousy, or hurt, but her lack of caring scared me.

"I didn't mean to lie." I sighed. "I really didn't want her. I never loved her."

"You slept with her while you were with me?" Katie looked at me curiously. "So you cheated on me?"

"Never." I shook my head vehemently. "It was after."

"After what?"

"We broke up." I took a deep breath. "It was the day you gave Harry up."

"What?" She frowned at me. "That doesn't make sense."

"The day you gave Harry up was the day I realized you were never coming back to me. It was the day I realized you hated me so much that you would have our child and give him up for adoption and never even tell me that I had a son." I stared at her through bleak eyes. "I hated you so much on that day. I hated you and I hated me and I resorted to something I'm not proud of."

"But she blackmailed you." She looked at me with a dazed expression. "Why would you sleep with her?

"Because I hated her as much as I hated myself." I shrugged. "I just needed a body—bodies. I just needed to be out of myself. To forget you and what we'd had. I needed to be with someone and use their body without care for their feelings."

"You did that to me as well." Her voice was soft.

"Never, Katie. I've never used you." I shook my head. "I love you."

"You don't know the meaning of love." She shook her head and closed her eyes. "All these years, I've been berating myself for doing something so stupid, for lying and losing the love of my life, but I think I should have been congratulating myself. I wasn't dumb. I was smart. You're crazy. You're self-obsessed. You only care about yourself. You're not capable of love."

"I love Harry, Katie. I'm a good father." My voice was terse.

"Yes." She nodded slowly. "You're a good father. A very good father."

"Can you forgive me, Katie?"

"There's nothing to forgive." She shrugged. "We both made mistakes. I think it's time we moved on. I want to be in Harry's life if you let me. I want him to know me as his mother."

"You're not going to run away?" I looked at her consideringly. "Now that you know everything, you're not going to leave and never look back like you did seven years ago?"

"No." She looked at me with clear eyes and smiled weakly. "I love my son. I won't ever leave him again. I'm not going to back down this time. I'm not going anywhere."

I fell back against the wall and burst into tears. I couldn't believe it. I couldn't believe that everything was working out the way I had dreamed it would. Katie stared at me in shock, and I walked over to her and pulled her into my arms, kissing the top of her head.

"What are you doing?" She pulled away from me. "Stop it. What's going on, Brandon?"

I walked back to the TV and turned it on again. "Look at the screen," I told her. "Look very carefully."

She looked at me in shock, and I pointed at the image of me.

"Look at the face. Look carefully, Katie." She stared at the screen for a few minutes and gasped.

"That's not you." Her face turned ashen as she realized the truth. "What is going on? That's not you!"

"Matt helped me put this video together." I walked over to her and grabbed her hand. "Let's go upstairs." We walked upstairs to my bedroom and I took her to sit down on the bed. "Maria went crazy when I ended things with her. He called me to warn me that he thought she was going to do something crazy. We have this video because, when I refused to pay Denise a dime, she hired someone who was my lookalike to pretend he was me. She took him to my apartment when I was out of town and set up a secret camera to record it. This was going to be her proof to the world." I shook my head. "I told you, she was crazy."

"How did you get it?" Katie looked like she didn't quite believe me.

"Matt got wind of it from a reporter he knows." I shrugged. "He pretended to be interested as a reporter, bought the video, and made her sign non-disclosure papers. It's been locked up for years, but Maria found it recently and well, I guess she decided to try and use it against me."

"That's crazy." Katie looked down at her lap, and I knew that now was the time that I had to let her know how I felt and what was in my heart.

"It's always been you, Katie. Don't you realize that? From the first day I met you, my heart has belonged to you. It's never gone anywhere else. I've just been waiting for you to come back to me."

"I don't know what to believe anymore." She shook her head and sighed. "Why didn't you try and get me back when we broke up? How could you do that to me?"

I grabbed her hands and stared into her eyes. "You were only eighteen, so young. I didn't want to trap you into a relationship if you weren't ready. I wanted it to be you who came to me. I wanted you to realize that I was the man of your dreams. The man you wanted to spend the rest of your life with. I waited so patiently, Katie. Every day, I sat by the phone, waiting. I didn't want to be the man who stole your youth if you weren't ready. When Will told me you were pregnant, I thought, 'This was it. This is when she's going to come back to me. She loves me and she's having my baby. There's no way she's not going to come back.' But you never did. When I heard you were giving away the baby—our baby—I hated you. I couldn't believe that you would give away a part of us. But eventually, I understood why. And I went and got him. And we've just been waiting for you to grow up and come back to us."

"I didn't know what to do. I wanted to tell you, Brandon. I really did. I was just too young. I didn't know how to tell you."

"I know that now." I took a deep breath. "You were too young and naïve and I was too old and set in my ways. I knew from the moment I met you that you were my forever love. But I didn't know if I was yours. I needed to know I was your forever love and not just your first love. So I decided to wait. I decided to let you grow up and do your own thing. If you loved me, really loved me, I knew you would come back to me."

"I've always loved you, Brandon." She looked at me

with passionate eyes. "That's why I got a job at a company I knew you were buying."

"The day you applied to Marathon Corporation was the day that my life turned back to color. I was so excited. I knew that this was the moment I had been waiting for. But I knew that I had to be more careful this time. I couldn't just welcome you into my open and waiting arms. I had to test you, Katie. I didn't want to hurt you, but I couldn't let you back into our son's life without knowing that you weren't going to run again. I needed to know that you were strong enough to go through hell and still come back to me. This isn't a game, Katie. This is for real. This is for love. This is for our life. I needed to know that you were mature enough to deal with a family. A real family. You've already broken my heart once and it killed me. I can't have you breaking our son's heart as well."

"I would never do anything to break his heart." She whispered softly.

"If you come into our lives and leave again, it would break me and it would break him. He's already forming a bond with you." I took a deep breath. "I didn't mean to push you so hard. I didn't mean to hurt you, but I had to know that you would stay, no matter how much I pushed you."

"Oh, Brandon. I'm not going anywhere." She leaned toward me and kissed me. "Please don't test me anymore. I'm sorry I lied about being eighteen."

"Katie, I want you to remember one thing." I took her hand and held it to my heart. "It wasn't that you lied about being eighteen. I can live with a lie. You were young and it happens. It was that you had so many opportunities to tell me the truth and you didn't. Even to that last day, you told me you were going to a business lunch. I knew there was no business, Katie. I just wanted you to tell me the truth. I wanted you to prove to me that, despite your age, you were an adult."

"You knew?" Her eyes widened and I nodded slowly.

"I always knew," I whispered in her ear. "Remember when I talked about being eighteen and first loves? Remember when I told you I was going to be a guest lecturer? Remember when I told you we could get through everything if we were just honest with each other? I gave you so many opportunities to tell me the truth. I so badly wanted you to tell me so that we could live our lives. But it wasn't to be at that time. You had to grow up."

"I can't believe you knew." She shook her head and I pressed my lips against hers softly. Her fingers ran through my hair and she kissed me back passionately. We fell back onto the bed, our hands exploring each other hungrily. I ran my hands down her back and under her top so that I could feel her skin. My fingers burned as they touched her and I felt a heat rising through me as she bit down on my shoulder.

"Wait just a second." I jumped off of the bed, ignoring the groans of my body as I walked to my closet and pulled out a small box. I walked back to the bed slowly, and Katie stared up at me with wide eyes.

"Katie." I got down on my knees and pulled her up so that she was sitting up and not lying down.

"Oh my God." Her hand flew to her mouth and I smiled.

"This isn't exactly how I had this planned," I laughed gently. "I thought we would be on a picnic somewhere and Harry would bring me the ring and stand behind me. I never wanted to do this in the bedroom or in the throes of passion. But I can't hold back. I don't want to hold back. I've never felt that a moment has been as right as this one is right now."

"Brandon." Her eyes glittered with unshed tears and I shook my head and smiled.

"I'm doing the talking now." I grinned as she rolled her eyes at me. "I knew I loved you from the first moment I saw you outside of Doug's, a place, by the way, we will never let our underage daughters go."

"We would never have met if I hadn't gone." She grinned at me and I gave her a quick kiss before pulling back.

"The day you came into my life with your gorgeous smile and your trusting eyes was the best day of my life. And our relationship was perfect. You were perfect for me. I was perfect for you. We were perfect for each other. I knew that in my heart. I always knew that. But I didn't want to capture a caterpillar in a jar and keep a butterfly hostage. I needed you to metamorph and come back to me. I needed to know that the beautiful butterfly had seen the world and knew that I was the one. And you came back to me, my sweet Katie. You came back to me, and all I want to do is hold you tight and never let go. I can't lose you again. I told you once that we were forever, that you were mine. I didn't mean that I owned you, Katie. I meant that you owned my heart. You were mine and I was forever yours. I love you. I've always loved you. Being without you for seven years has aged me more that you'll ever know. Marry me, my darling. Marry me and make me the happiest man in the world." I opened the box and slowly took out the ring I had bought for her all those years ago. "Will you marry me, Katie?"

"Yes, oh yes. Oh, Brandon," she gasped as I slowly slid the ring onto her finger, love emanating from my every pore. I pulled her into my arms and kissed her all over, feeling like I had finally won. Everything had finally come together and I was finally going to live the rest of my life with the woman I loved with all my heart.

***

I watched Katie and Harry playing with his new train set and felt content and happy. This is what I had been waiting for these seven years. I walked back to my office with purpose. It was time now. I could get rid of all of the documents Will and Matt had given to me.

I grabbed the key from my pocket and opened the safe, pulling out the files that were sitting there. I sat back and stared at the first file Will had given me seven and a half years ago, when I had first met Katie. I listened to Katie's laughter and smiled as I shredded the documents.

"Daddy, Daddy! Come and play with me and Mommy." Harry ran into the office with a huge smile on his face and happiness in his eyes.

"Just a minute, son."

"Okay." He rolled his eyes at me and I laughed. He looked just like his mother when he did that.

I stood up and looked at the final document in the folder, feeling a sudden release of pent-up emotion. This was the first piece of information I'd ever gotten on Katie, from a couple of days after we met. It was the information that could have and should have ended everything. I stared at the machine as it gobbled up her birth certificate and walked calmly back into the living room to spend time with the two people I loved the most.

"Who wants to play a board game?" I asked casually, sliding my arm around Katie's waist as she relaxed into me.

"Me, Daddy! Me!" Harry jumped up and ran to his room to get his games.

I laughed before whispering in Katie's ear, "Don't worry, my love. Tonight we can play our own games."

Katie's hand slid to the front of my pants and she grinned wickedly at me. "Who says we have to wait for tonight?"

THANK YOU

Thank you for reading The Ex-Games. There is a new series called The Private Club featuring, Meg (Katie's best friend) that is connected to this series. You can get part I here:

http://www.amazon.com/gp/product/B00IA9TB2G?ie= UTF8&camp=1789&creativeASIN=B00IA9TB2G&linkC ode=xm2&tag=offtheshe-20

To be notified as soon as the next parts are released, please join the J. S. Cooper Mailing List by going to: http://jscooperauthor.com/mail-list/. Also, please feel free to like my Facebook page: https://www.facebook.com/J.S.Cooperauthor for more updates.

If you enjoyed this novella, please leave a review, and recommend it to a friend.

OTHER BOOKS BY J. S. COOPER AND HELEN COOPER

The Forever Love Boxset (The Last Boyfriend, The Last Husband, Before Lucky)
Scarred and Healed
Crazy Beautiful Love
The Rich Boys Club (The Billionaire Men of Romance)

CPSIA information can be obtained at www.ICGtesting.com
Printed in the USA
LVOW10s1001210615

443286LV00020B/1382/P